THE MOTHER MUST DIE

First published in 2024
Published by Puncher and Wattmann
PO Box 279
Waratah NSW 2298
www.puncherandwattmann.com
web@puncherandwattmann.com

Cover art: Rosie G
Cover design: Miranda Douglas and Rosie G
Text design and typesetting: Miranda Douglas
Editing: Ed Wright
Proofreading: Claudia King
Printed by Ingram Spark

ISBN 978-1-923099-34-0
A catalogue record for this book
is available from the National Library of Australia.

This project has been assisted by the Australian Government through Creative Australia, its principal arts investment and advisory body.

THE MOTHER MUST DIE

Koraly Dimitriadis

Puncher & Wattmann

For Maroulla

Also by Koraly Dimitriadis

Love and Fuck Poems

Just Give Me The Pills

She's Not Normal

Contents

Geographical reference: the following stories are set in Australia where the word 'wog' has a different context to the UK. 'Wog' was used as a racial slur against the Australian Mediterranean migrants but was reclaimed in the '90s with the highly successful and acclaimed 'Wog comedy' genre, such as *Wogs Out of Work* and *Acropolis Now*. The term is acceptable to be used within such groups in Australia.

This is a work of fiction. Unless otherwise indicated, all the names, characters, businesses, places, events and incidents in this book are either the product of the author's imagination or used in a fictitious manner. Any resemblance to actual persons, living or dead, or actual events is purely coincidental.

1.

They Put Me In My Grave

I'm so angry, man. They put me in my grave. That is what they did—the two of them—they put me in my grave. I did everything for them. *Everything*. And her? She did not lift a shoe from the floor in our house for the whole twenty years before she marry. I kill myself for her, for all of them. I cook, I clean, the only thing I did not do for her—forgive me to say—is chew her food and shit for her. I give my whole life for them all and what do I get? I get shit, that is what I get.

When she bring him to me, unrefined as he was, I ask him. I say to him if you take care of my daughter I will look after you forever, and you know what he say to me? He say, 'I promise to take care of your daughter forever'. I *promise*. The words of the young people today, they mean nothing. This generation, they have it all prepared for them, laid out on the bed nice. They not know work. If I take them to my days in the village let's see if they survive. My mum had six children and we look after each other because she sick all the time. In my day a promise means promise. Not promise and then I change my mind. You know what I should do when he say this to me? I should say to him 'bullshit'. That is what I should say.

I took care of him, from the moment he say this to me I take care of him. I have no sons. He was my son. I call him my son. *Yie mou*. He call me 'Mum'. I treat him like my own. I treat him like a prince. Elizabeth, she was lucky to have someone like him take her as a wife. *Kilingira*, always lazy, she was. He was a good boy—he cook, clean, help my Elizabeth. I am good like this. I know a good person, I can *smell* if something is no right. I am like a *drako*. Dracula. He was good. Tell me one man who do these things for his wife? I don't know one. But *I* was the one who taught him the right ways. Do you think he would be the man he is today if he did not have me to teach him? I don't think so! He did not even know manners at the table. An only child. *We* taught him family. He did not know family before us.

His Maltese father leave when he was a young boy. And his Polish mother—from the moment Paul love my Elizabeth she did everything to cause the trouble for them and for my family. She drink the wine every night and yell for the neighbours to hear and then they even stop to see her because she no stop being crazy. She say her husband, Paul's father, hit her and all these other things, but I no believe anything that woman says. Who knows what she did for him to not see her child. Excuse me to say, but if I was her husband I would probably leave her too.

She throw Paul to the streets when he engaged with my Elizabeth. I say to him I will look after him if he look after my daughter and he look me in the eye and promise me. He said: *I promise*. So I look after him. I open my house to him. He sleep in the spare room (not with Elizabeth, of course). I even make him sandwiches to take to his work. I cook for him, I wash his clothes—I was his mother. My husband was his father. He did not know what father was. I bring him into my family, to my sisters, the cousins, everyone they love him. And now they have both made us an embarrassment. A *rezili*.

I did not mind that he was not Greek. I was happy that my Elizabeth was happy. She spend the year before only in her bedroom. She no go nowhere. So when she meet him I say to her: go, be happy. Okay, my husband say to her 'no boyfriends, just friends'. He too strict, I understand this. But we only try to protect her from the Australian monsters. Australia is not Greece, it's scary, man! And nobody force her to marry. *She* say she want to marry him. *She* want to marry him not me! Now she say to me she did not do sex with him. She with him for ten years. Ten years! But how she have two babies if she no have the sex? I no understand this. Who tell her to marry a man she no do sex with? Not me! And she telling everyone this *now*? After they have the children? Did she not think of all these things *before* she have the children? When you have a child you have responsibilities. You can no just say 'I want to leave'. Men are shit, everyone knows this. But when you have responsibilities, you have responsibilities. You think I no want to leave sometimes? When I was young and my children were little, I think to leave. But then I go to the library and read a good book about why you should stay. It was the best book I read and it saved my life, my husband's life, and my children's life. It save us all.

I don't want to see Paul's face now. I don't want to see hers either. When I see her face all I think is what she do to me. When I see him I just want to cry. Life is over for me now. It is over. I don't even want to leave the house. Ever. I'm staying here and I will die here, in this house. Did I not deserve a holiday for all my hard work? I go on my holiday with my husband and you know what I come home to? Shits. Shits is what I come home to.

They both lie to me. Did it take them ten years of marriage and two children to realise they did not want to be together? Why did they not tell us from the start? They lie to us for ten years. I go on my holiday to Greece to see my family, to go to my mother's grave—*o Theos na tin anabafsi*, may God rest her soul—and she calls me and says she is not living in her house anymore. She leave 'to find herself', she say. If she was in front of me I would take a hammer to her head. Then she did not see us for six months. Six months! She change her phone number, we not know where she is. We only see Paul. He bring us Felicity and Ross. He tell us he try to fix the things. Poor man. He try and try. A man cannot survive on his own. He has needs. I don't blame him for finding that *koloaftsraleza,* Australian bum, he lives with now.

Elizabeth was so stupid. She tell him to give her money and he can keep all the things in the house. It was not even that much money, $5,000. If Elizabeth had the smallest bit of brain she would not accept the money and take the things. But her brain is like the seed of a fig. And now where is she? She left with no clothes on her back. No job. On the government money. Renting! She did not even take the Kenwood Mix Master! The walls are cracked in her little flat. I don't go there because when I do I want to die. I want God to come and take me. I can't. She had that big house in Ivanhoe, the swimming pool. We go and tell everyone how proud we are of her and now look what she's done. Look. She had a husband work for her, help her in the house. She had everything. And now she has nothing.

This is what promises are. No respect. And then they want to sell the house and they get the lawyers. I tell them, and my husband tell them, the lawyers will suck the blood from your veins until you are only skin and bones. They say it on 3XY Greek radio every day. Don't go to the lawyers. Don't go to the lawyers. But do they listen? Why would they listen to *me*? I am nobody, right? And they still continue now with the lawyers and with the custody. They think the children can be cut in half with a knife. They are children, not dolls. And they do not stop. And now all the money they have—which we help them to get that money, by helping them—all this money, it go to lawyers. Why don't they just come to my house, pull down their pants, and shit right in my living room. Why not? It's the same thing.

They had all the things in that house because of *us*. We spend the money on the wedding, this is the custom. He had only ten people. We did the wedding three hundred people. We go to the weddings and give money at every wedding so people come to our daughter's wedding and give us money and gifts on the registry. I work hard to take care of the children and my husband worked like a black man to make the money to give our girls a proper wedding—we come to Australia with only the clothes on our back! We pay for the three hundred people and they come and return the happiness to us that we gave to their children when they married, and now my Elizabeth is left with no house, and he sits in his new house, with his new woman—oh yes, she is clever the new *koloaftraleza*.

I tell my Elizabeth he would not wait for her to stop her stupid behaviour. I tell her that a clever woman would snatch him before she could blink and I was right. Because I know. I know these things. She go to Greece and my sisters put some brains in her head and she come home and ask him maybe they try again but it too late. The *koloaftraleza* was already in. He is the stupid one—she has four childrens! Why he no find a woman with no childrens I will never understand. He could find a nice woman but instead he go find that bulldog Australian. He work until the night doing his job and she look after the children. Yes. If you give me a million dollars I look after your childrens. I will drive the *Mercendez* and have the nice clothes and not worry about the money and shut up. I would like to sit with my legs up and no worry about the money. So why she not do it? I would do it. I no think she is stupid. She is smart. She is smarter than my daughter, that's for sure. This is love. What you think love is? There is no love in life. There is only bullshits. Bullshits and money. There is only commitment. Commitments and love it not the same thing.

Elizabeth lives the free life now, but what about all the shits she leave behind? She goes where she likes, does what she likes, but *I'm* the one paying. Me. And I will take this pain with me when they bury me and only God himself, when I go to him, will understand my pain. It was all for nothing. All my hard work, my sacrifices, for nothing. I don't want to have anything to do with anyone. I will look after my grandchildren when they ask me, but I am not twenty years old. I am fifty-five. I won't be alive forever. They will not know what to do when I am gone one day. And I *will* be gone. Soon. Do you think I have many years in me? I don't think so! Some days I need to take two Voltaren just to make it from the start to the end of the day. Felicity and Ross pay too. They are the ones who pay. Me and them. Elizabeth and Paul, they are living the free divorced life and Felicity and Ross they treat them like dolls they carry from one house to the other.

We were up with the birds to make it to the church service today. I'm not one of those people who attends the festival only and doesn't pay my respects before. We are celebrating Apostolos Andreas the saint. We must do the right thing *before* we celebrate. This is the logic.

Me and my husband, Yianni, we going to Apostolo Andreas church festival. Yianni is driving. He always drive because I no drive to far places, only in my suburb, Epping, to the shops to get the groceries and things.

It be nice if Elizabeth and Dimitra could come but Elizabeth can't because she had to be in the hospital a few days ago. She had a procedure to clean out her woman parts. She is staying with us because she have nobody to look after her. But this was *her* choice. Of course I take care of my own daughter. But it's not easy. It's not easy when every time I look at her I want to break her bones.

It is going to rain today. I know it. The sky look angry, like someone kick it. The storms are coming.

The church is packed out, man. I no expected so many people. Geeze. Lots of young people. It good to see them. They have more respect than my Elizabeth. She won't go into the church anymore. She say the church 'scar' her, or whatever she say, 'give her fear', but this is bullshits. This is what I mean. It is very hard for me.

After the church, Yianni is talking to some friends and I tell him I go and buy some *koubes*. They are like—what you say—fry meatball with herbs and things inside. Dimitra and Elizabeth they want me to bring them some. They are nice but I prefer the *shamishi,* which is like a fry pastry with the custard. It is a sweet you have with the icing sugar on top. But even the *shamishi* today tastes like—excuse me to say—shit, after everything Elizabeth put me through. Life is just shit. It is very shit.

'Hello, how are you?' It's Salomi, second cousin to my cousin. She is smiling. But it not a real smile, it is a sticky nose smile. I don't want to talk to her. I don't want to talk to anyone. I have not said to anyone about the divorce and it be two year. It's too hard for me.

We speak in Greek.

'Hello,' I smile. We kiss on the cheeks.

'How is Elizabeth?' she say, like she worried. 'Toula said she is not well.' She wiggle her nose like she is trying to vacuum the gossip with her nostrils.

'She's good. Oh, there is Yianni. He's calling me. We will talk later.'

Toula said she is not well—what a joke. Women they have nothing better to do than stand around and talk about other women's misery. I look around to find Yianni. He is talking to some other men. I don't know why I come here. I want to just stay in my house. It is all Yianni's fault. He never take responsibility for the childrens. Everything is always on me. He busy himself with the Greek community and having coffee with friends and I get stuck with all the shits.

I don't talk to him in the car. I'm so angry, man. The Greek radio is playing old songs. They play a song my mum she used to like. I miss my mum. I no see my mum much after I leave from Greece when I was nineteen. They had no choice but to send us. No money to marry us. We have to come here and find a husband. We had to go, we couldn't complain. There was no room to complain. But I'm happy I come. I hate to go back. It's too hot there. No, Australia is my home now. I have my childrens and my family and I need nothing else.

She is on the couch when we come home, talking with Dimitra.

'Did you bring *koubes*?' Dimitra ask.

'Yes,' I say. 'And *shamishi*.'

'Yum,' Dimitra say.

I look closer at Elizabeth. She crying. Again.

'Anyway, he's a loser,' Dimitra says to her. 'Try not to think about it.'

Elizabeth blow her nose on a soggy tissue. 'When is my life going to get better though? Why is it so hard?'

I go to the kitchen to start the dinner. I already defrost the chicken. I'm making roast chicken with potatoes and sweet potatoes.

'You've just had surgery,' Dimitra say. 'Just relax and try not to think about the future. Everything will get easier.'

'Hmph,' I say from the kitchen.

'What was that, Mum?' Elizabeth shout.

'I say "hmph" because you should think of these things before you divorce.'

'Can you shut up, please?'

'*Stamadiste*,' Yianni say.

We all listen and stop, but I no want to stop. I want to say. I have a right to say and speak. But I don't. I don't say anything. I keep it in. That is my job isn't it? To shut up and take all the shits? Isn't it?

When we have the dinner, Elizabeth is not eat much. She cry in her plate. I see the tears fall from her eyes.

'We forget the yoghurt. Dimitra, *mboris*?' I ask.

She nod and go to the fridge to get it. But at the table when she open it she disgusted and say, 'Oh, yuck, *ehi* mould *bano*!'

'*Boo*?' I take the yoghurt and there is the mould. I look at the date. It is expire tomorrow. I take the yoghurt to the sink and start to take the mould out.

'Mum, what are you doing?' Dimitra ask.

'It is just mould. Someone must accidentally put food in and it grow mould but it's okay. You can eat.'

'I'm not eating that,' Dimitra say.

'*Oi re, den ithete ftohia esis*.' They have not seen poverty, I tell them in Greek.

'I don't care. I'm not eating from that yoghurt. It's disgusting. Is there another one?'

I shake my head.

'Great. Like I said, there is never any food in this house. I don't get it.'

Now there is no yoghurt. I no feel good that there is no yoghurt. I don't say anything.

After dinner I make a plate for my Australian friend Jane next door and give it to her over the fence. My friends are the old people. I like to talk to the old people. Everyone else, including my sisters and brothers, they give me the shits.

After, we all watch the *Big Brother* on television. I can't believe Sarah kissed Claudio after what he say to her in the spa last week. She should no kiss him again. While I watch, I go on the phone and type back through the Viber to my sisters in Greece. I send a new photo of my roses too. I go on the Facebook program too. Some people on the Facebook, it's like they are sitting all day putting the photos. Don't have anything better to do? And they think I have the energy to sit all day and look—I don't think so. I just search through fast and then I close.

Elizabeth is still not talking much. She only say she is hurting and the pain killers not work. She say she go to bed. Felicity and Ross will come to our house tomorrow from Paul's house so maybe then she be happier. But that is more work for me, of course. If she still be married with Paul then he look after her. She needs someone to look after her.

'I'm going to bed,' she say.

'You okay?' Dimitra ask.

Elizabeth no respond.

'Dimitra ask you something,' I say.

'I'll be okay when my mum stops making my life a living hell and starts supporting my choices and supporting me.'

'I no supporting you right now? You stay in my house. Is this no support?'

'Yeah but at what price?'

'If you expect me to be happy you on your own now then you be waiting a long time because this will never happen.'

'You know what? I am a mother and if my daughter was going through what I was going through I would support her and not badger her every five minutes. Do you have any idea what that does to me?'

'What about *me*? What about what *I* am going through?'

'What *about* you, Mum? This isn't about you, this is about me.'

'No, it's about *me*. All my life is been about you! I work hard to raise you and marry you—it was no you father. He be at work and I do all the work and I wait to marry you so I can rest and have my time—my time to be about *me*—but now I start all over again. When is my time to rest?'

Yianni get mad and go outside for a cigarette but I no care. I will say what I want.

'You are destroying me, Mum.'

'No, you destroy you.'

'And then you wonder why I got married in the first place.'

And she go off to bed. I hear her cry as she go. She thinks she the only one that cries? I cry too. I cry in my bed too after Yianni sleep. I cry for my mum.

I am in the kitchen when she wake up in the morning. I say to her, 'Good morning.'

'Is it?'

'I pick some roses for the garden today. You see all the colours.' I show her the vase on the table. 'This one is my favourite, the orange one.' I'm proud of my garden. I love my garden. It is the only place I feel calm.

'Yeah, they're nice.'

'Are you hurting today still?'

'Yes.' She start crying. She start crying a lot. I sit next to her.

'Why you cry?'

'Because life is shit.'

'Tell me about it. I been saying this to you all my life.'

She laugh. But then she cry more.

'So we do the best we can with the shits,' I add.

'How?'

'You look in front and you no look behind.'

'You don't love me.'

'What is this stupid thing you say!'

'You don't! It's been almost two years since I split with Paul and you act like you hate me and you have not even hugged me, once, once, in two years.'

'I'm you Mum. Of course I love you.'

'Then say it. Say you love me. And hug me.'

'You hug me.'

'No, Mum. *I* am the child. I am *your* child and I am asking you, who gave birth to me, I am asking *you* to hug me and tell me you love me.'

So I stand up and I hug her. So strange to hug. My mum never hug me. Elizabeth cry in my arms. 'Of course I love you, *beli*.' Silly girl.

'I love you too, Mum. I'm sorry I'm divorced. I'm sorry.'

'It's okay, life is shit, what you do?'

And we both laugh and cry.

She have the breakfast and we talk more. She ask me why we no talk about the sex when she was young. I say to her we did talk about the sex: I tell her the sex is to do when you marry, that is all you need to know of the sex.

'But you never hug and kiss Dad in front of us.'

'Not me, your father. I told him.'

'But ... I mean ... do you have sex? How often do you have sex?'

'When we got married it was more of course, but now not as much because we are not so young anymore. Maybe once a week?'

'What?! Once a week! But you're always fighting.'

'Okay, sometimes twice.'

She laugh some more and then she lie on the couch. The doorbell it ring. It is Paul. Yianni goes to answer but I tell him I go.

'Hi, Athina, how are you?' Paul say. He say 'Athina' now, no more 'Mum'.

'Good, Paul, you?'

'*Yiayia, Yiayia*!' Felicity and Ross hug and kiss me and run in. Felicity say to her dad, 'Come in, I want to show you something, Daddy.' She pull him inside to the living room. Then she run to her mum and hug her. Paul say hello to Yianni and Dimitra, but he no say nothing to my Elizabeth. Nothing at all.

'Excuse me, Paul. You no see Elizabeth there on the couch?' I ask.

'Yes.'

'So why you no say hello to her? She is right there.'

'Hi,' he say to her.

'Because I thought maybe you didn't see her and that was why you no say hello!' I laugh.

He look at me like he can't believe what I just say. Not just him, but all of them. But I just say the truth, that's all. I think they expect me to say some more but I just wait for him to speak.

'Oh, nah,' he say, quickly. 'Anyway, I better go.'

He leave soon after and it start to rain outside, just like I say it would. I told you, I know these things. It start raining some more, heavier and heavier. It is going to hail, I tell them all, and of course, I am right. But then more hail it come and more and more. We all go out on the veranda. Wah! Hail! Hail I never before seen in my life. The whole yard it turn white, like when it snow in my village. The gutter is overflow.

'Oh no, this is no good. My garden! My garden!' I say.

'Dad, the walls are leaking,' Dimitra shouts and she run inside with Yianni.

The yard it drowning. Only me and Elizabeth are on the veranda watching like we can't believe. I shake my head at my garden. 'Forget it. Forget everything. It's over. Destroy.'

'Yep,' Elizabeth say, and we laugh and smile at each other.

2.

Conquest

It's lucky I turned out smart like my dad and not stupid like my *nonno*. One day, all of this will be mine. This is what I think every time I walk into The Roma with my woman on my arm. Tonight the club is packed, the DJ's spinning the latest techno tunes, and everyone's partying on.

My dad owns two clubs, The Roma and The Venezia. He's worked hard, built up a clientele over the years, and now our reputation supersedes all the other bars and clubs in the city. Our clubs are upmarket. They're not for scumbags, they're for people of quality. The Roma is three floors. It's got ten massive crystal chandeliers—they're not even fake—the place is decked out in black marble with statues like you'd see in Roman museums.

Dad started the clubs in the late 70s but they keep going from strength to strength. But clubs aren't his only thing. He's got his fingers in all sorts of different pies. Dad's worth millions. All the family works in the business—uncles, cousins, my sister, my mum—everyone. It's important to me to help my dad build his empire up. That's what being smart is all about: knowing what's important.

I never met my *nonno*, and I probably never will. He might even be dead, who knows. When I was young, around seven, my dad sat me on his knee and he told me about my *nonno*. *Nonno* lived in Rome and he was a bloody rich man. He had land all over the place—in the villages—growing fruits and vegetables, rice and grains, and all sorts of other shit that was in demand and exported around Europe. He had lots of labourers who he paid practically peanuts—they would take anything he gave them—that's how poor they were. *Nonno* had a wife and kids (my dad and uncles and aunties). He had it all. When he strolled through a village, people would flock to him, and they'd kiss his hand like he was a Holy Man, that's how much power my *nonno* had. But the thing was—and Dad explained this many times to me and my siblings—my *nonno* was stupid. He had all this power but he was fucking stupid.

My dad never told me what *Nonno* did, all he said was he did something so stupid the police were after him and he had to split. As I got older, I thought maybe it was drugs, but Dad would crack it when I asked so I never pushed it. My dad, he didn't see his dad after the age of fifteen because *Nonno* never came back. When he turned eighteen, he sold his share of the estate, packed his bags for Australia, and never looked back.

My whole life my dad's been telling me not to be stupid like my *nonno*. When I'd go out with the boys instead of doing my homework he'd yell, 'Louie! Are you going to be smart like me or stupid like your *nonno*? What's it going to be?' Of course I'd say smart like him. Like I would want to be stupid like my *nonno*.

The club is busy tonight. Everything's running smoothly. I slide my arm around Monica's waist, brush her long blonde hair aside to talk into her ear. She smells delicious. 'What would you like to drink, babe?'

'Can I have a cosmo, babe?'

'Sure.' I kiss her warm cheek. We're extra affectionate with each other today because of the Tiffany bracelet. What can I say, I like spoiling my woman. It's dangling and sparkling from her wrist like a declaration to everyone that she's mine. And there's more to come. The engagement ring is ready, all that's left is to smooth out the creases with the family. I don't care what they say anymore, I'm not going to let them stop me. Monica is the woman I want. She's the only woman

I've been with who gets me. She makes me want to be a better man every day I'm with her.

I wave a waiter over.

'Boss, what can I get you?'

'A cosmo for my beautiful woman, scotch on the rocks for me.'

'Coming right up, boss.'

Monica's friends arrive and the girls are jumping up and down at the bracelet. I use the opportunity to slip away, tell Monica I'll be back in a minute. I weave through the crowd, make my way out the back to the office. Dad's crunching numbers behind the desk, just like I knew he would be.

'Louie ...' He doesn't even look up at me.

'Dad,' I say, and I say it firm, so he knows I'm not taking no for an answer, 'I'm here with Monica—'

Straight away he's up, pointing at me hard like I'm some kind of crim. 'Me and your mother we already said—'

'I already got the ring—'

'You go with other women and you want to *marry* her?'

I want to shout the apple doesn't fall far from the tree but don't. 'I don't *do* that anymore.'

'I told you from the start when you go with her I would not accept this.'

I turn away from him, grab at my mouth hard, because I need to look away from his face, I can't handle his face. There's a tear forming in my left eye, I blink hard, suck it back into where it came from. I take a breath. 'Dad,' I begin slowly. 'I want *her*. I love her. Please. I want to be good, honourable. Don't you want me to be happy?'

He scoffs. 'Love? I do not care about love. I care about family. You being stupid like your *nonno*.'

'How?' I implore him, 'tell me how? I have done everything you wanted me to do. I studied what you wanted me to, I am in the business, at uni because you wanted me to—what more do you want?'

'We will not accept an Australian in the family,' he says, pounding his chest with pride. 'Blood is what is important, and my blood and the blood of my family will stay pure and true to my country.'

'I'm doing it, Dad.'

He moves from behind his desk, comes over to me. 'If you do this,' he warns, and I know he's serious because he's speaking right into me, his stance unwavering, unaffected by my pain, 'I will write you out of the business. You will not be my son. You will be out on the streets, begging like scum. Listen to my words: you will be out. You decide if you want to be smart or stupid. Now get out.'

I challenge his threat with my stare. I want to strangle him. I want to take my hands, wrap them around his fat Italian neck and I want to squeeze so tight until he's got no air.

I do what he says. When I get back to Monica, she's sitting in the booth reserved for us. My scotch is on the table. I scull the whole glass.

'Babe, you okay?' Her hand is on my shoulder.

'Yeah.'

She kisses my cheek, gets back to chatting to her friends. I wave down a waiter. He's serving someone else. He's taking too long. Why is he taking so long? I go up to him. 'When I waive you down you come straight away. You hear me, cunt?'

His eye sockets bulge. 'Sorry, boss.'

'Get me another scotch, and make it a double.'

'Coming right up.'

It takes four months of solid commitment, but finally I get my list back up to scratch. Ninety-seven is my golden number. I used to keep the names in a notebook, but for motivation I typed them up and now I have the entire list on my phone.

I'm fucking proud of my list. If I can't remember a name afterwards, I write 'unknown'. But lately I'm trying not to do that. Lately I want names, because that's what I want, and that's what I'm gonna get. Okay, so things slowed down when I was in a relationship but now I'm back to my pre-Monica days and things are looking up.

I don't answer her calls. When the image of me telling her 'it's over' ventures into my mind I punch it out, then I down it with a whisky for a final thud.

'How long are you going to keep letting your family run your life?' she yelled, and her hair was a mess, her makeup was all smudged, and me, the cunt, I did nothing. I just stood like a fucking statue and I couldn't say nothing. So I said nothing and I did nothing and she just wouldn't stop crying so I left.

She's been blacklisted from the clubs. Dad got my sis Leanne and my cousin Tony to pay her a visit a few weeks ago, just to clear the air. They gave her their sympathies, explained in a nice yet direct way that the family wanted her to stop calling me, to stop bothering me. She hasn't tried to call me since. That's the best part of my family. We stick together like super-glue, and we can never come apart. That's what family is. Family is just money and fucking glue.

I know my mates are stoked I'm on the prowl again. My Friday and Saturday nights are with them. We get shit-faced at one of the clubs, chat up the girls. Drinks are on me and at the end of the night I always end up with a chick on my cock. Another name for the list. Boom. Score. Then afterwards I catch up with my mates and we talk about our conquests and what we made the chicks do.

It's Saturday night and we're at The Roma in a booth and I'm telling them about my fuck last night and how she said she didn't suck cock and I said 'get your fucking head down there, bitch,' and I pushed her head down and she did it. I love the sound of the rowdy roar of my boys after one of my stories, the celebratory chink of scotch glasses coming together, makes me feel like I'm the king of the world, just like Leo in the Titanic

What else are chicks good for anyway? Housework and fucking. I don't know what's going on now with this women's movement, sounds like a load of shit to me. Men have cocks and women have pussy. We are meant to fuck *them*, not the other way around. Men rule the world, end of story. If you don't like it, just stay home and clean like my mum.

I'm eyeing a hot, thin, black girl across the room. She smiles at me. I smile back. She looks fresh, catwalk supermodel type. Her friends are pretty hot too but she's the one I want. Probably hasn't had much cock in her.

'Excuse me, boys. Time for another conquest.'

I head in her direction, and as I'm walking I lightly brush past her. 'Sorry ...'

She giggles. 'It's okay.'

'I'm really sorry. Hey, can I buy you a drink to make it up to you?'

'No, it's alright, thanks. I don't really take drinks from strangers.'

'I'm not a stranger, I own this club.'

'Yeah, right.'

I place a hand on her shoulder, gentlemanly—I'm all charm. 'If you don't believe me, let's ask one of the waiters.' I wave one over. They come instantly. 'What's your name?' I ask the waiter.

'Bob.'

'Bob, can you please tell this beautiful lady if I own this club?'

'Yes, he does.'

She looks amazed. 'Wow, really?'

'You see? Now what drinks can I get for you beautiful women?'

It doesn't take much effort to get them comfortable in the booth with us. Sandy's the name of my chick. I get chatting to her, act like I'm really interested in her life and school and blah blah but all I can think is my cock's getting hard. I keep the drinks coming and coming until we're laughing about I'm not sure what, and there's a hell of a lot of touching and flirting going on.

'Hey, do you want me to take you to our VIP room?' I ask.

'What's the VIP room?'

'Just a chill-out room, for very important people.'

'Okay!'

I take her by the hand, lead her through the club and out the back to dad's office. Nobody's around. I close the door behind us.

I start kissing her. She likes it. Our tongues meet in my mouth. 'Where's the VIP room?' she says.

'I lied. There isn't one.'

I kiss her again. We go deeper into it this time. I press her against the closed door, slide my hands up her skirt.

She tries to wiggle away. 'Let's go back to my friends …'

'Nah, more fun here …'

'Come on …'

I press into her more. 'Tell me how you like to fuck.' I spin her around so she's facing the door, grab at her arse.

'I'd like to go back …'

'Don't pretend like you don't like it.' I undo my belt, get out my cock. I pull up her skirt, move her undies aside and rub her with my cock. She's wet. I knew it. That's why girls wear skirts, to make us fuck them. That's what they all want. And they like it rough. They pretend they don't but they do. I put my cock in her cunt, bare back, and fuck her. I come on her arse.

When I finish, I zip up. She's still pressed against the door, like a sticker on paper. I rip her off by the elbow. I get my phone out of my pocket. 'See this?' I say. She's looking at the ground. I lift her head to see my phone. 'It's my list. Now I'm gonna add you to my list, Sandy. Or better still. You type it for me.'

I hand her the phone. Her hand is shaking. She types her name. 'Can I go back to my friends now?'

'Go.'

She leaves. By the time I get back to my mates she's gone.

When the coppers come to our house a week later, the first thing I think is someone's caused shit down at the club. But when they tell me they want me to go down to the cop station, Mum, Dad and Leanne look at me like 'what have you done now?', and I don't know why they're giving me that look for. Obviously there's been some mistake. But I don't want no trouble so I say I'm going down there and Dad says he will meet me there with our lawyer, Vito, who is a friend of the family.

I've never been out the back of a cop station before. They put me in a room that stinks of foot odour. There's double sided glass. When Dad comes in with Vito I say, 'I didn't do nothing, Dad.'

'Are you sure?' he asks.

'Yes.'

'Okay, I believe you. We will fix this.'

Two coppers come in. They introduce themselves but I couldn't give a fuck what their names are. They look like toy soldiers, all stiff and righteous. The Australian kind. Then one of them says something about sexual assault and rape and my Dad and I look at each other, and my Dad's face—even though he is just nodding and listening to the cops—I can see through his eyes his heart being crushed, and it's like I got my hands in his chest, blood and all, and I'm the one doing the squeezing, and even though I feel like I'm going to chuck my guts up, a part of me relishes in the massacring of my own father. In that moment, I want him to die.

'I'm going to be sick,' I say.

'We'll get you a bag,' one of the cops says.

They're saying they need my DNA. I need to give them a DNA sample.

When the DNA matches, I get arrested. It's like the movies when they come to pick me up from home, they cuff me and put me in the back of a divvy van. Mum and Leanne are crying. It's like a fucked up joyride in the back of the van. I have to stay in the city cop station until my case for bail is heard by the judge. Thank God they keep me in my own cell, away from the loons, but I feel like I'm just hanging on, like my crazy is just about to snap.

That stupid bitch. Maybe I should show the coppers my list. Like I need to force someone to have sex with me. Anyway, Dad will sort it out. Okay, it's a small cell, ok the food tastes like garbage, but I can do this. Fingerprints with the ink. Photos. Procedures. Who does she think she is messing with? She doesn't know who I am. Who my family is. I told the coppers already, that I thought she was into it, that I had no idea she wasn't into it because she never said nothing. But the cops were talking about consent, if I asked her or if I just did it, and then Vito advised me not to answer that question. Dad was quiet. He's barely said two words to me since all this. I want him to yell at me, to tell me I am stupid just like *Nonno*, but he doesn't. He just talks legal stuff.

At the hearing, Vito makes me sound like a top bloke, explains to the judge about how good a character I am, how I run the business with Dad and that we donate to all these charities, like the Children's Hospital, Red Cross, Salvation Army, to the council, to the Italian community. The judge sets the bail to $100,000 and Dad pays it straight away. I can go home. Finally. I just want this nightmare to be over.

Vito comes over for coffee that night and says we need to get some strong character references. Dad mentions the head of the Catholic parish, the mayor, the Italian consulate general—all friends of the family. Dad says 'no problem', we can get the references.

'There will be a trial,' Vito explains, 'but as long as he says he believed there was consent, he should be safe.'

When Vito leaves, Dad hands me the newspaper.

'What's this?'

'Look on page three.'

I unfold the paper, turn the page. There's a photo of me. The heading says 'Son of Alberto Abruzzo accused of sexual assault'. I can't help it, something inside me cracks, and suddenly there's water coming out my eyes. I'm crying like a stupid girl. Everyone is going to find out now. I need to clear my name. That stupid bitch! If she was here right now I'd stick my hand down her throat and rip her guts up. Black piece of shit.

'I'm sorry, Dad.'

'You shame my family. You poison the blood of my family, just like your *nonno*.'

I wipe my eyes. 'N*onno*?'

He shakes his bunched fingers at me. 'He did this, your *nonno*. You did exactly like him. He was doing it all the time. He thought his money would protect him, but one day he be with the wrong woman. He had to leave and never return but you will not do the same, you will fix this, you will clear my name and the name of this family!'

'But, Dad, I'm innocent!'

He grabs me by the shirt, 'You will fix this,' he yells in my face, and the tears explode out of me, can't control them, and for the first time ever, an uncontrollable fear spreads through my entire body. God, help me!

3.

Cypriot Blue Skies

Vicky is running—fast. Away from her other self. Strapped into an aeroplane, she is flying among the cushiony clouds. They are the buffer, the padding, separating her from all she wants to leave behind.

The two halves of Vicky do not understand each other. They are not of the same age. They do not dress the same. One is naïve, underdeveloped. The other has worn bones and responsibilities. They do not walk the same or act the same. *Pull.* They pull away from one another. They tear. Tear in half. Tear like a page. Run. They run away from one another.

On the inside, Vicky is crying. Her teardrops are like sad Greek love songs. On the outside, Vicky functions. She exists. She carries herself eloquently down the path she was destined to walk. One foot, then another foot. But inside she is screaming. She screams like a hundred Greek tragedies in chorus, their echoes vibrating in her almond-coloured eyes.

Then Vicky arrives. And the other half of her is nowhere to be found. This is how it always happens. It has vanished. It is gone. Vicky continues on her path. It is sunny now. It is not the bitter, unpredictable, Antarctic cold she escaped, the place she was frozen into like an ice sculpture. Here it is Cypriot sunny, like the glow of an angel. The warmth is descending on her, melting all of the ice beneath her surface, in and around her heart, so she can fully break free. There is a light wind. Limassol, the city of wind. She is walking the historic, medieval old town. Narrow paths weave in and out. There are only a few people around. It's so quiet, faint voices only, somewhere in the distance. She likes that there is nobody around. A scooter tears through the solitude then disappears.

Vicky continues on. The corners of her mouth do not curve down like they usually would. Her face is light and smiley. Vicky is happy. This is freedom to Vicky. Her feet are firmly planted in her soul's home. Warm, hot sun, sauna heat. Freedom. There is anticipation in her step. Everyone knows everyone here. Everyone is interconnected in one way or another. Maybe she'll run into him. Maybe he'll be happy to see her. Maybe she'll cry. Maybe he will too. You never know who you'll bump into on Cypriot streets. No need to stress when you will see someone. Just have faith. Go slow. Cypriot slow. Rushing is bad for you. Go slow, Vicky. *Slow*. She likes the pace, she likes the space. There are no people pushing up against her, demanding things from her. Nobody demands anything here. Aphrodite's medicine lingers in the air. Breathe it in. Absorb it. It heals.

Along the path, around a bend, a little girl appears like an apparition. She says *Mum. Mum. Mum.* She calls Vicky 'Mum'. The little girl hugs Vicky. Vicky hugs her back. Vicky loves her. They hug, tight. They make a noise when they hug. A murmur. A sigh. Soft love. Sigh. Love. Belong, sigh. The little girl takes Vicky's hand. She pulls at it. *Mum*. But Vicky isn't sure. The little girl yanks. *Mum. Mum.* She pulls with the strength and weight of Australian lands, with the authority of Vicky's husband; with the obligation of her other half. The little girl is pulling her back. The little girl knows. She knows Vicky's truths. She knows there are two of her. Cyprus pulls Vicky in the other direction. They pull. Pull. Pull apart. Mum. Vicky is a mum. She is a mum pulled apart. She was married too young. Vicky is not free. She never was. But she needs this, to be *here,* to hide so nobody can find her. She yearns to fly like a bird into pale-blue Cypriot skies, fly until it is night and she is no longer visible.

Vicky breaks away from the girl. Vicky runs. Runs, *runs* in her free flowing red dress—the wind pulls at it. The little girl's cries haunt the wind. Vicky runs, her heart burns. Vicky yearns for love. Love that tastes like the cherries hanging on the trees in her grandmother's village. Love like touch. Young, first love touch. Love lips, passion, first love passion. Unreserved passion. Vicky loved like that once. She can still feel the kiss on her lips. The rush through her body.

Vicky arrives at the Mediterranean shore. The colour has vanished from the sky. Stars burn bright. The air smells of sea salt. Vicky makes her way into the water. The red dress becomes heavy like the ache in her chest. But she must proceed. The ships in the distance bare witness. Vicky dives into and under the sea. Her eyes are closed. She hears her daughter's shrill. It travels to her from distant Australia. Her daughter is in her bed, shrilling in the night. *Mummy. Mummy*! Vicky opens her eyes. She is not in the water anymore. She is not in Cyprus. She is in a cold house. In Australia. She is laying on the couch. It's 5:38pm and darkness is descending, grey and pink haze. She is not wet from the sea, she cannot smell the salt. There is not a spec of sand to be found. Her face is wet with tears.

4.

Blood-red Numbers

Who says you can't have everything? I want to have it out with that person, yell in their face, beat them down, obliterate them. Who says I can't have that wad of cash and eat pussy too? I reckon you can get high on the scent of cash—on that smell of too many thumbprints sweating over that bank note. My dead Serbian father taught me that. He taught me what money *means*. One day I won't have to carry credit cards. I'll have so much cash in my pocket you won't be able to tell the difference between that and my hard cock.

A mansion in Toorak sounds nice. A Ferrari—red, shiny, smooth. That, and to command the attention of a room just by walking in.

I like the title *Head of Technology*—I like it a lot.

I prefer *CEO* but patience must be exercised.

My reflection stares back at me. It's looking into my eyes.

I am young. I am young, attractive and important.

Attractive, young, corporate.

Swallow with entire face, force down the lump. There is swaying, unnoticeable to the eye, but enough to cause mild nausea. These are the effects of over-confident mingling in the clouds, fifty floors up from the Earth's surface.

Shake myself off, adjust tie, and exit men's room, black shoes tapping and important against polished, timber floors.

In the open room with floor-to-ceiling windows overlooking Melbourne's skyline, humans disguised as corporates dangle elegant glasses filled with expensive fluid. Trays float on the hands of tired waiters dressed in white, wearing rehearsed smiles. The room is buzzing with the reward of food. Smoothly integrate into a conversation with colleagues, chatter and smile, eat and chatter, but the food does not fill the hollowness as expected. Strange. A waiter presents a sausage-roll platter. I take one, dip, bite ... what is that? It tastes like ... *blood*? I gag, choke—they watch me with bewilderment. There's no choice but to swallow. Smile at colleagues, all of them strict followers of the cult that is corporate. Strict.

I am them.

There's Bob—Head of Technology. Mid-forties Aussie Bob is a big guy (width-wise), has no wife, no family, and attends all work functions. He's by the window, is looking out at almighty buildings shooting up into the endless orange sky. He is high on corporate finger-food. The lights in the buildings burn bright, melting the planet, employees working all weekend to meet that deadline. Employees like everyone in this room. Should talk to Bob, make sure he hasn't forgotten about our meeting tomorrow. It is of importance in the corporate paradigm, where everything lost will be realised.

Clear my throat, swallow the blood and head over. Extend my hand, a firm handshake to emphasise my keenness in climbing the ladder in this billion-dollar bank. Schmoozing takes place, words of work, project deadlines and share prices, but soon the conversation dries up and we're left nodding and swaying, eating and nodding.

Are you still in touch with Tania?

I have to blink at his words. Loosen the strangling tie around my neck. *Are you still in touch with Tania*? What the fuck, what the fuck, do I still see *Tania*? The urge to pick up a chair and smash it across Bob's head compounds. Dig fingernails into my palms instead. How utterly moronic to mention ones ex-wife at work. But this isn't technically 'work', is it? This is a work *function* which employees are *expected* to attend in their *own time*. Ha! The mockery of 'own time'! The myth of *time-in-lieu*, invented by corporates to brainwash fresh students plucked ripe out of university. 'Own time' is theirs for the taking! An employee who believes otherwise and refuses to work more than their contracted hours will be punished with poor performance appraisals. Promotions and pay-rises are withheld for the worthy. And strict followers that relinquish rights to 'own time', they will frown at the non-conformists, their faces contorting, stilled like a photo.

You okay, mate? Bob is scratching his head.

Then a sudden change, the lights in the buildings outside switch from white to red. Numbers begin to pop up all over them *{12.31 87.95 55.34}* and so on and then the red, it's streaming down the sides of the buildings like blood. Clench fists harder to stop myself from ramming Bob through the window, want to smash the glass, make the numbers disappear, watch him freefall fifty storeys down and splatter on the Bourke Street footpath. Shake my head to erase the numbers. No luck.

Here, sit down, I'll get you some water.

Sit on a chair. *Mate, drink this*. Bob hands me water—gulp it down.

Tomorrow, *mate,* tomorrow I'll get what was promised. Smashing you through the window would be a CLM (Career Limiting Move).

Take a deep breath, smile. *I'm okay, thanks.*

Back at my apartment, three streets from the office, the numbers come again. Have they always been? There is no way of telling. I have memories with Tania when I was numberless. But I can't tell for sure. Tania appears in my dream surrounded by numbers, a pointy number one through her chest. There is a computer, lines and lines of jumbled Java code, red numbers *Public Class Invoice {65.90 65.45} String money {78.96 56.44}* and I am pounding the backspace key—DELETE—but they don't erase, the numbers get bigger and bigger, fill the entire screen, electronic blood seeping from technological overuse.

I wake in a sweat. Down King Street towards Vic Market, I pay for pussy, cover her face and pretend it's Tania.

It's still dark when the alarm wakes me. Dress like a robot in snazzy suit, pretend it's Armani. *One day, one day*. You have to visualise your end game. Want it. Invent it. Today will be like all the other days, got to get stuff done, in by seven-thirty out by eight, ten, or maybe I'll finish my work at home, accidentally stay up all night, and life will become one endless work day. But it'll get quieter, after this deadline or the next or never. No worry—there's nothing ten cups of coffee can't fix.

{76.54 86.45 77.65}

Fuck off, numbers!

Swipe in at seven-thirty like all the other drones, clutching briefcase. Walk past Graham and Tracy (Graham's work-wife) and they're engrossed in an important 'work' conversation. I saw them fucking in the photocopy room once. Graham's got a wife and two children on the outside. No time to gossip. Big meeting today. My performance appraisal. Documents are up to scratch, spent hours creating spreadsheets and Word documents to prove my worthiness and billable time over the past six months, and productivity, and extra hours (two-and-a-half of me) but it's all for a good cause: me, my career, promotion, big bucks, up the ladder, mansion in Toorak, sports car. I'll get promoted. It's all done, sorted. Need another coffee.

Sit on ergonomic swivel-chair located in my space, a desk separated by a mini-partition wall in an open-plan area where phone conversations can be heard. Switch on my two computers. One day I'll have an office like Bob and the head-honchos that smoke cigars. My mini-partition wall is barren apart from the memorandum of 'Core Values'. *Inspiration* will be applicable today. *Inspiration*. Once there was a photo of me and Tania. Fuck people. Today the praise bestowed will bring it all into equilibrium. Click, click on the mouse and open up Java interface. Start coding, fingers dance on the keyboard.

Sometime later, Bob yanks me out of code world and into his office. Spread my documents out before him but he proceeds to speak without acknowledgment. His words are distorted, jump like a scratched CD, and the numbers take over *{12.67 77.87}* blaring like red neon lights.

You took a bit of time off with your divorce and I didn't feel that you met your targets.

Push the papers closer to him without speaking, blinking hard at the numbers but they're relentless *{5.43 87.09 9.66}*.

You know how it is with the bell curve, mate. We can't promote everyone and William put in the hard yards the entire six months.

The numbers are screaming *{4.09}* screeching *{5.78}* ringing in my ears *{9.72}* contemplate Bob's guts *{4.01 2.02}* on steam-cleaned corporate carpet, but not just him, all of them who decide fates at a round-table while smoking *{1.54}* cigars.

Killing Bob would be a CLM.

Instead exit his office without a word, make myself a boiling hot coffee, take it to my space and drink without a squirm. Code and code and my fingers cramp but push through the pain and just like the dream the numbers come up, red and alert *{1.09 2.12}* but don't try to erase them and still code and code. *Private static void main(string[]*

args) {*1.01 2.32 4.10*} Java, Java, try block with a catch, catch all possible exceptions in program to prevent billion-dollar bank from debiting incorrect account because that would be *bad*, really *bad* of me to do that to the bank that *respects* me, that *acknowledges* my hard work and determination and *sacrifices* {*3.66*}. Smirk, then chuckle, and two of the strict ones frown so I halt, but still laughing on the inside at the thought of media spectacle, of damaging the good-Samaritan image of the bank that donates to charity and is so *generous* to humankind. It may even decrease shareholder value.

It's dark outside already and my butt aches from sitting. Head space is fuzzy and requires a large dose of sugar. Scoff down Burger Rings purchased from vending machine placed strategically in common area for empty shells like me. Stare at empty partition wall, restless at the absent photo. Want to cry but understand crying is for girls but just to see her face again would be nice, smell her sweetness, and maybe it wouldn't be classified as stalker-ish or {*1.11*} insane if our photo was reinstated and I pretend we didn't break up because she asked me to choose. *Me or work*, she had said, *me or work, me or work ...*

Bitch. Need more cunt.

Take a walk to King Street, come back rejuvenated. Remove naughty bit of code in the program. You can't have everything in this world, but you almost can if you *wait*.

My time is coming.

Two weeks of takeaway dinners later, it gets worse.

An announcement is made at the monthly meeting where food is served alongside bottles of booze, only nobody eats and everyone's really still, although I want to fidget, fidget {*0.12*} squeeze my shaky hands together but can't *{0.05}* control the fidget, want to fidget, want to fidget, want *{0.02}* want *{0.11}* to, want *to f-i-d-g-e-t*. It all started with Bharat six months ago. When he arrived from the Bangalore office Bob reassured us he was here to help. The aim was to create a team, like in the 'Core Values', and there was no reason to question. But a head-honcho has just announced that most technical jobs will be moving to India. Three Indians equal one of us. It's all about being competitive, increasing shareholder value, buying up market-share to dominate the world. Of course, you can imagine *{0.12}* the numbers *{0.34}* at this stage *{0.01 0.23}* raging wild *{0.01}* insane.

No. No. They would never get rid of me after all the sacrifices, *never*.

I have two lots of pussy that night.

There's no job, no job, no job, just fucking, lots of fucking, and smothering of faces not Tania's. Bob told me in his office. There were words. There was me, sneaking in after-hours and inserting the naughty code. There was me, getting caught. Now there is just … just me wandering … wandering the streets in the night. Somewhere in the mass of tissue in my head, memories shoot off, but then they get trapped in a cloud of compulsive, consuming tear-at-your-skin-and-make-it-bleed-buy-a-shotgun-off-some-street-dude anger *{0.81 0.64 0.04 0.00}*. There are just numbers now. They are at the stock-exchange. The greedy, head-honchos in America that smoke cigars made it happen.

The stock exchange, it's calling me. That is where I must go.

The thirst for numbers is demonic. Too many faces at the Collins Street building, too many, blurred in with the redness. Soak in the bloodbath of numbers. They came to me as a premonition. It is my responsibility. But, wait, hang on a minute, there's a yellow number and then … a *green*. Green? Green! No. No green. They must all be blood-red.

There are old men, two of them, talking of America injecting millions of tax-payer dollars into the economy, bailing out Wall Street giants. Apparently our Prime Minister followed like a lost mutt. The cigar smokers in Toorak are laughing. I can hear their cackles, their phlegmy coughs. Laughing at the gullible government, at the pensioners, at me. They're waiting for their million-dollar handshakes.

The cigar smokers must die.

Take myself and the new gun to Toorak.

5.

The Recipe For Sweet Cherry Flan

Voula knew she would have to be quick. Teresa was occupied in the make-up section, separating her lashes with a mascara brush; but Tony, he was stationed outside the chemist, and he had not switched off the car engine. Voula could hear the pounding of music emanating from his Commodore. She knew peak hour traffic on Sydney Road would be backing up against his patience.

She approached the prescription counter, clutching her pink walking stick. What was the name Teresa gave it? Oh, yes—helping hand. It was as pretty as a walking stick could be, a gift from the family to remind her she was no grandmother at forty-nine. Not that Voula was ever one to wear makeup and parade. She did not fear looking her age. Time had been kind. Her chestnut curls were far from grey, and she certainly did not look as if she was the mother of two adult children.

Her gaze crossed with that of a woman her age. Voula pressed on. She could feel the woman trying to make sense of her. Soon the stick would be discarded, she told herself. Soon.

Voula reached the prescription counter and took a rest. Her muscles exhaled.

'Mum, what are you doing?' Teresa was beside her. Voula did not like Teresa's attitude when she chewed gum.

'*Na me perimenis* exo.'

Her jaw stopped. 'Why? You know if I go to the car without you Tony's gonna crack it. We got the Panadol, let's go.'

'Akous ti leo?'

Teresa spun to the exit. The doors sprung open for her.

Voula closed her eyes and breathed. She needed to be more careful with her words. The children were suffering enough. She would have to try harder.

'Mrs Papadopoulos—is there anything else I can help you with?' He was lovely, Mr Tranter. Always helpful.

'Yes,' she said gently. 'I need information about a medicine. It is called Iplex.'

'Iplex? I don't believe I've heard of it.'

Why did her legs feel weaker today? Maybe it was just her imagination. 'Can you look in your compuder, please? Maybe—'

He smiled, but something about the flavour of it didn't feel right. 'Mrs Papadopoulos, I've been running this pharmacy for fifteen years. I think I would know if—'

She took his hand and he stopped. 'Please look.'

He cleared his throat. 'Alright,' he said, taking his hand back.

Voula smiled. 'Thenk you. Please look.'

Anticipation was in the air. It was Orthodox Easter and Voula was throwing one of her renowned *trapezia*. Leading up to the dinner party there was always talk on the family grapevine: 'I wonder what *Thia* Voula's cooking' or 'I hope she's making her cherry flan.' And the comment that would infuriate the other mothers: 'I hope *Thia* Voula's making *basticho*. Her *basticho* kicks ass over my mum's *basticho*'.

Voula had called Teresa twenty times that morning to raise her from bed and into the kitchen. Voula may not have been able to reach the stove to deep-fry the *keftedes* that day, but she prepared the mixture, with the grated potato, chopped parsley and just the right hint of cinnamon. She retrieved the ingredients by wheeling herself around the kitchen on an office chair. Her hands moved from the kitchen bench, to cabinet handles as she pulled herself this way and that.

When Teresa finally made it to the kitchen with her hair pinned up, she multi-tasked between dishes as the clock ticked closer to arrival time. 'I do not understand you,' she flustered to her mum in Greek. 'You should not have had this party.'

Voula's hands squeezed through the mincemeat mixture. 'I have you to help me.'

Teresa slid the tray of potatoes into the oven. 'You like to cook. Me, I don't like to cook. And I have study.' Teresa shook her head, switched to English and said, 'If the relos knew the truth they wouldn't let you have the *trapezi*.'

Voula sighed, resting her hands in the bowl. 'Tomorrow, you can study. We will have leftovers so we won't have to cook. Don't make things more difficult than they have to be, my Teresa.'

'This *trapezi* is making things difficult.'

Voula gave her comments a dismissive wave. 'Come, this is not the time for arguments—the meatballs.'

Teresa rolled her eyes and stepped to the stove.

'Each meatball must be the same size.' Voula rolled a *kefte* in her palm.

'It's all gonna end up in the same place.'

Voula handed her the *kefte*. 'Presentation is everything.'

Teresa lowered it into the pot of oil—it sizzled.

'Stop picking on Mum.' Tony entered from the backyard.

Teresa turned to him. 'What did you say, idiot?'

Panagioti followed Tony holding oversized, metal skewers for the lamb on the spit.

Tony continued to the fridge—Teresa's eyes followed. He retrieved the bowl of marinated *souvla,* placed it on the bench.

'You're one to talk,' she continued. 'You know Mum's not well but do you help around the house? All you care about is clubbing.'

'Stop,' Panagioti warned in Greek, peeling plastic film from the bowl.

Tony stepped towards her. 'I've got uni *and* I'm researching Iplex.'

Voula patted Teresa's arm. 'Come now, we all have our roles to play.'

Teresa and Tony glared at each other.

'Oh, and I don't have Year 12?' Teresa rebutted.

Panagioti's fist slammed the bench. 'Stop!'

Anguish sprang from Teresa's eyes. She turned back to the stove.

Life isn't fair, Voula thought. Why was God doing this?

Panagioti rubbed his forehead. 'Voula, you are doing too much. You must go and rest. Teresa will finish the cooking.'

'I'm fine.'

'No—'

'No!' She clenched her fists. 'This is my house and if I can do something let—me—do—it.'

'The doctor said—'

'I don't care. I'm finishing!'

Silence.

And so, they resumed their roles, Tony and Panagioti threading *souvla* through the skewers, Teresa and Voula frying *keftedes,* the hum of the rangehood dulling the space between them.

The house was a disarray of greetings, overdue conversation and excitement. There were bunches of flowers, trays of cakes, laughing children and too much to say. Kisses were exchanged, Easter wishes, *Christos Anesti.*

'How are you, my sister?' Yiota asked Voula. 'How is the leg?'

'Better today,' Voula said.

Yiota approached Teresa.

'Hello, Aunty, how are you?' Teresa forced a smile.

Yiota did her usual dramatic nod, clutching her lower back. 'Yes, yes, the same. The pain is there, but life, it continues.'

Teresa raised her eyebrows. 'Anyway, I better get back to the food.'

'Yes, tell me what needs to be done.' Yiota tied an apron, joining her sister Angela and the clang in the kitchen.

The queue formed quickly at the kitchen bench when it was time to eat. The younger children sat in the living room, some distance from the parents and older children, who sat in the kitchen. Angela distributed traditional red-dyed, hard-boiled eggs. The phrase *Christos Anesti* was repeated as pairs cracked eggs to determine the winner with the unbroken egg.

Voula motioned Teresa to her. Teresa came, knelt by her chair. 'Can you please bring me my food?'

'What food?' Yiota asked as she took a seat beside Voula.

Teresa and Voula exchanged a quick look then Teresa went to the fridge.

'What food?'

Voula watched Yiota's two grandchildren cracking their eggs. 'I am …' Voula cleared her throat. '… dieting.'

'Nonsense. There are no diets for Easter.' Yiota stabbed a piece of souvla, plonked it onto Voula's plate. 'Eat.'

'Yiota—'

'Mum, I can't find it,' Teresa was beside her again. 'I asked Tony to check the fridge last night for leftover organic vegies. He said he did.'

'It doesn't matter …'

Teresa scanned for Tony. He was across the room cracking eggs.

'We will make do …'

When he caught Teresa's gaze, Tony ignited, came straight over, knelt opposite Teresa.

'What did I do now?'

'Did you check Mum's food last night?'

'Yes. There's *fasolakia yahni*.'

'They're not organic! I wanted you to check if there were *louvyia* because they were organic.'

Tony looked Teresa hard in the eyes, so hard that his began to water. Voula tried to take his hand to stop him but he was too quick and before Voula could believe it, he was making his way towards the front door.

'What is happening here?' Yiota asked. 'Where is Tony going?'

'Shut up!' Teresa snarled at her *Thia* Yiota. 'You complain about your back and your this and your that when you've got no bloody idea!'

An uncertain silence occupied the room. The ruckus noise of the younger children in the living room jabbed, once, twice, until they too were affected by it. Everyone looked at Teresa with confusion. Voula assessed her, the way she stared at the tapestry of Greece on the wall, and the dread poured into Voula, filling faster and faster until it reached its brim when Teresa covered her eyes with her hand and sobbed.

'I'll go after Tony,' one of Voula's nephews said.

'Leave him be,' Panagioti sighed. 'Teresa, come and sit by me.'

Teresa shook her head. Her uncle Gregory went to her side and embraced her. 'What is it, my Teresa?'

Voula tried to stand, to reach for her, to stop her, but she knew she couldn't, she wouldn't make it in time. 'My Teresa, please don't …'

'I can't, anymore. I love you, my Mama …' She turned to Gregory. 'Uncle, it's not her leg only. She is unwell.'

Gregory turned to his sister. 'What is it, Voula? Is it serious?'

Teresa continued to cry into her uncle's eyes.

'Is it serious?' Yiota repeated.

'No.' Voula surveyed the room with short, panicked, movements. 'We don't know for certain.'

'What is it?' Angela asked.

'Look at me! I am fine. Tony is finding me medicine. Iplex. It will all be okay. Please stop, all of you.'

But they wouldn't stop. They kept asking and talking, trying to make sense, wanting to talk to Tony, asking for Tony, talking one above the other until Voula couldn't take it:

'Stop!'

All talk ceased.

'Please. Let us enjoy our meal and later, the children can go home and we can talk. Alright?'

They all looked at each other.

One by one they picked up their forks.

It was the slowest they had eaten at one of Voula's *trapezia*.

Voula's three siblings, Angela, Yiota and Gregory, sat in the living room with her that night. Their spouses stayed too. Everyone else was gone. They were all waiting for Tony. Tony would have all the answers. Tony would fix everything. As the eldest, he was always finding out and explaining things Voula and Panagioti could not understand. The children of migrants often carried the burden of communication. Voula didn't like this, she felt guilty for it. But nothing could be done about it. It was the reality of living in Australia.

Teresa served tea and Greek coffee. Angela and Yiota sat stunned as

Panagioti explained motor neuron disease (MND) as best as he could, a watered-down version of what he understood when Tony explained it to them.

The rattle of keys outside the front door jolted their attention. Tony walked in and stopped. 'What's going on?'

'They know,' Teresa said from her post beside Voula.

He shook his head. 'Know what?'

'About Mum.'

'You are so ...'

Teresa's tears re-emerged. She hugged her mum.

'Tony, sit,' Gregory pleaded.

Tony leaned against the wall. 'It's MND.'

'How do you get this?' Angela asked.

'From chemicals,' Panagioti said bitterly.

'Toxins, Dad, and they haven't done enough research to prove that. It could be a virus, genetic, stress on the body ...'

'It is chemicals,' Panagioti said.

'What chemicals?' Yiota asked. 'Have you been near chemicals, my Voula?'

'No.'

'Nowadays,' Panagioti continued, 'everything we eat has some sort of chemical on it.' Panagioti paced the room, delving into theories on household cleaning products, aluminium foil and drug companies. 'The medication we take when we are sick, it treats one problem but causes another. They want us to be sick, to make money.'

'This is nonsense,' Angela said.

'Eee.' Panagioti shoved a palm in her direction. 'Your brain is full of spaghetti.'

Voula sighed. 'Panagioti, please.'

'Is this illness related to the leg problem?' Gregory asked Tony.

Tony nodded. He explained everything: how motor neurons control muscle movement in our bodies but in Voula's case they are slowly dying off and her muscles are wasting away. He explained the progression of the illness, that Voula would have accidental falls, eventually be unable to walk, that it would be harder to swallow, talk, but he would not venture into the nightmares that would follow. Voula insisted she felt fine, and Tony emphasised the hope, an experimental drug Iplex he'd been researching that hadn't been released in Australia yet. It was developed for children who couldn't grow but someone with MND had tried it and it had stopped the illness progressing.

Their faces brightened.

Gregory shot his arm through the air. 'We will get it!'

'Uncle,' Tony sighed, 'this is where the situation gets complicated. When Iplex was found to help MND, the small company that produces it was taken to court by a very big, powerful company.' Tony tried to explain it plainly: when a drug company creates an ingredient, they own the recipe to it. One of the ingredients in Iplex is this big company's recipe. But Iplex also has another ingredient and it is those two ingredients combined that can help MND sufferers. Because of these recipes or 'patent laws', the big company won, withdrew Iplex from the pharmacies, and replaced it with a drug that doesn't help MND and costs $10,000 a month.'

'But when can we get Iplex?' Angela asked.

'Soon, I hope. There is a study in Italy that is using Iplex and another in the US. It's just a matter of time before it comes here.'

Gregory nodded. 'I will call Thanasi tomorrow. His daughter works for the drug companies. Certainly she will be able to help.'

'Tony will find a way.' Angela smiled towards Voula. 'This is why they make drugs, to help people.'

The family buzzed with talk of Iplex. There were letters sent to drug companies, to the Australian and Italian governments. There was talk of emails and conferences with associations, applications for EU passports. There was enthusiasm over findings on the internet, special herbs or diets that MND sufferers had tried, particular treatments that helped certain people.

Apart from overhearing conversations, Voula never asked how far away Iplex was. She trusted Tony and was happy to busy herself with cooking, cleaning and her job at the nursing home.

It had been four months since Voula had been stationed at the reception desk. Her role of twenty years had changed from caring for the elderly to paperwork and greeting the visitors. They told her it was not safe for her to be taking care of people with her leg as it was.

'Voula, so good to see you.' It was Rachael, Frank's daughter. Frank had been in the home for two years now. Her face was pale and she had nice blue eyes like her father.

'Hello, Rachael,' Voula smiled.

'Dad says he hasn't seen you in a while. I didn't know you were at the front.'

'Tell him I will come and see him then.'

'Okay, I will.'

She would have to go when nobody was watching. She didn't want the questions and the looks from the managers that accompanied her requests to visit residents. She told Larissa, who sat with her at reception, that she was going to the bathroom. Voula stood, and as she walked with her helping hand across the hall for the bathroom, she, ever so carefully, looked over her shoulder, saw Larissa conversing on her phone, then quickly and methodically did a ninety-degree turn and began for Frank's room.

It took her a while, but she got there.

Frank couldn't stop laughing and talking. 'I was wondering where my favourite lady had got to.'

'You better be careful, Dad, or Panagioti will be coming for you!' Rachael joked.

Voula had overstayed, but she would deal with the consequences later. She was just too happy to think about anything else.

'So your leg's on the mend?' Frank asked.

'Oh, yes, won't be long.'

'I told you, Rach, she's a tough one this one.'

Voula would have to hurry back. She would have to concentrate and hurry. But when she stood her legs were not cooperating. They seemed impartial, defiant. She said her goodbyes and pushed forward. She would have to get back. She didn't want the questions and the analysis, and everything, she didn't want any of it. Voula was halfway down the hall when her legs somehow became tangled.

'Voula!' It was Tracy, her manager. Voula held on so tight. She did not want to fall. She did not want to hurt. 'It's okay, Voula. Let's go to my office.'

'I'm okay. I'm okay.'

'It'll be okay. Come on.'

She knew as she sat in Tracy's office, watching the cup of tea Tracy had made for her steam on the desk, Voula knew what Tracy was going to say. It wasn't the first time Voula had almost fallen. Tracy's lips moved, but all Voula could hear was a droning hum. She couldn't take a word in. Panagioti came to pick her up. Tracy and Panagioti spoke. Then they went home.

A few days later, Panagioti came home with a Sudoku puzzle book. 'To help pass your time,' he said.

She pushed it away. 'I don't want it.' Voula wheeled herself to the back door, down the little ramp they had built for her office chair and onto the veranda. He did not come out. She did not want him to. Voula began to cry. She cried for her family in Greece. Voula wanted to get to know her parents as an adult. She had not done that. She had only seen them twice in the last twenty years. She longed for days in the village running around the family plantation, hiding behind the cherry trees with her siblings.

Voula closed her eyes and imagined the taste of the cherries.

Her siblings visited regularly. Conversations changed from work and house chores to memories and the past. They laughed a lot. It was the one positive of her illness, the sitting down and talking about life and the things that mattered. Sometimes when her immediate family couldn't take her to a doctor's appointment, one of her siblings would. At first she didn't mind the help, or when Angela and Yiota ironed Panagioti's shirts, or dusted. But the day Angela brought a casserole dish of food, Voula wanted to explode.

'What is this?'

'I brought some dinner.'

Voula turned her cheek to Angela's kiss.

Angela stood back. 'What is it?'

'I can cook my—own—food.'

Angela placed the dish on the bench. 'Please don't be angry. You need to rest.'

'Do not tell me what I need.'

'I see you how you struggle to stand, my Voula, do not pretend with me. You have to face reality.'

Voula stared at the tapestry of Greece, the tiny stitches her mother sewed with her swollen, aged hands. 'I am.'

'Then why do you not buy a wheelchair? The office chair is dangerous but you insist on using it. You are unwell, and the more you push yourself—'

'Your food is not welcome here. Please go.'

Angela sighed. She took the casserole dish. 'I will call you.'

Voula did not answer her and so she left.

That afternoon when Teresa came home from school, Voula had put the argument with Angela to one side. She had the Greek radio playing and was enthused about the evening ahead. 'Go and study. I will cook tonight.'

Teresa wasn't convinced as she bit into the apple she had just taken from the fruit bowl. 'But how are you going to reach the stove?'

'I can pull myself up. Go.' She shooed her from the kitchen. 'I will call you if I need you.'

'Thanks, Mum.' She kissed her mum. 'I'll be in the study if you need me.'

Voula hummed Greek songs as she wheeled herself about the kitchen. Although the energy seeped from her each time she pulled herself to standing, the textures of the food, the vine leaves, the stuffed peppers, the smell of the spices intertwining, fuelled her.

When she was almost done, Tony arrived. Voula wheeled herself to the living room. 'My Tony, are you staying for dinner?'

He turned on the television. 'I got a thing—hey, before I forget—'

'Well, look who it is.' Teresa stood with her hands on her hips. 'Decide to make an appearance?'

'Shut up—Mum, I want you to visit a doctor so he can see if you're okay to fly to Italy for the Iplex study.'

Voula had never been to Italy. Would she see the Colosseum, or the tower that leans to one side? But then the tiredness dampened her enthusiasm.

'What the hell?' Teresa said. 'Are you like, crazy? You don't even know if she can get into the study.'

'We have to try,' Tony said. 'Why don't you even want to try?'

'I don't want to put Mum through it all, that's why! I want her to enjoy the time she has, not travel around the world looking for cures that might not even work!'

Teresa stormed towards the back door and burst into the backyard. He followed. The screen door slammed behind him. They continued to argue. Voula wheeled herself to the kitchen. All that was left was to put the *yemista* into the oven. It would require some manoeuvring but she could do it. Their voices escalated. She wanted them to stop fighting and just love each other. She needed to find a way to tackle this problem. Every problem had its solution. She would find the solution to this one. Voula pulled herself up, the Bessemer dish resting on her forearms—but then one of her legs wobbled ... softened ... she tried to grab the oven door without dropping the dish—she couldn't—the food flew from her arms, splattering stuffed vegetables across the floor.

Her body cracked to the diamond-tiled floor.

She screamed.

'Mum! Mum! I got Iplex!' It was Tony. He was running towards her clutching a small vial, tears glistening down his face ...'

Voula opened her eyes. She was in a hospital. Panagioti stood over her, smiling. He took her hand, brought it to his lips. 'How are you?'

Voula cleared her dry throat. 'What did the doctor say?' but the words had to be forced out. Panagioti was quiet. She searched his swollen eyes, and she knew, she knew. 'I don't want the wheelchair,' she cried, shaking her head. 'I don't ...'

There were only chocolates in a box. That is all she could offer her visitors while recuperating at the rehabilitation centre. There was no coffee, no cherry flan. She would be there for three months.

She couldn't go to the toilet by herself, bathe or dress. Nurses occupied the space around her that she wanted empty. Her muscles twitched, her limbs were stiff. But it was her voice that troubled her. It was unrecognisable to her. Talking required so much more effort. Sometimes she closed her eyes and concentrated on making it sound stronger, confident. But the more she tried to tighten her grip on it, the further it slipped away.

'I'm sorry, Mrs Papadopoulos,' her doctor said in the presence of her immediate family. They were in her tiny room. The warm sun sliced in through the window. 'The disease is progressing rapidly.'

'This doesn't change our plans for Italy and Iplex,' Tony said.

'And what's Iplex?' he asked.

'It's a drug that can save my mum.'

He closed Voula's file, brought it to his chest. 'Well, I've never heard of it. Your mother needs physiotherapy, not a 20-hour flight.'

'Of course you've never heard of it. Doctors should learn from their patients.'

The doctor stood taller. 'I do not condone medication that hasn't undergone a full clinical trial.'

Tony smirked. 'You doctors have no clue.'

'Tony,' Panagioti said.

Tony remained fixed. 'If it was as easy as conducting a "trial" I'd borrow money and fund it myself. But we both know it's not about trials, so please don't treat me like an idiot.' Tony walked out.

Pou 'ne ta hronia? Where are the years?

She could hear her brothers, the ones in Greece, playing bouzouki to the Dalaras classic. This is what she would think as she sat in her wheelchair on the back veranda of her house with her Sudoku book. Over the past month, she had graduated from the easy puzzles and was now onto the medium ones. The family called her 'Champion of Sudoku'.

The puzzles helped. They stopped her from staring at walls and thinking. They helped when she couldn't stop crying. On horrible days when there was no elevator at a new doctor, or when a doctor told her unpleasant news, they were comforting. She no longer left the house except to visit doctors.

When she wasn't doing puzzles, Voula hovered around the kitchen.

Teresa was at the sink peeling potatoes.

'Let me help.'

Teresa jumped, pressed on her chest. 'Mum, you scared me.' She grabbed the bowl of potatoes, banged them on the bench. 'There.'

Voula stared at her lap. How she wished she could relieve Teresa of all the household duties; relieve her of this hell.

Teresa chopped an onion on the board.

'This is not how to cut onions.'

Teresa looked out into the nothingness in front of her, exhaled. 'Who cares how I cut onions?'

'Me.'

Teresa put down the knife. 'Okay. Show me.'

'Bring me a plate.'

Teresa brought Voula a plate, onion, and knife: Voula cupped it in her palm then cut it elegantly in half. She married one flat half with the plate, ran the knife down its length five times. The onion was then rotated and the cuts repeated.

They were perfectly diced onions.

'Thank you.' Teresa took the plate. She chopped on the bench.

Voula wheeled herself to the potatoes. She lowered the bowl onto her lap. Her hand moved to the peeler—but it refused to close around it. She blinked a few times to erase the moment and tried again—it was as if the gripping action had been unlearnt. Her breath quickened. She tried again and again and finally managed a weak grip. She moved the peeler to the potato, pierced the skin—the peeler skidded across the floor.

She looked up. Teresa saw everything.

'Mum?'

Voula lowered her gaze to the potatoes. 'I think I will go and rest.'

Voula didn't have much time. She was home alone expecting Yiota. She wheeled herself to the cabinet where they kept the phone book, lifted the hefty volume onto her lap and opened it to the pharmacy pages. She rang the first on the list.

'Hello? Can you speak louder?'

'Can I talk to chemist?' she forced out.

'Please hold.'

Music. 'How can I help you?'

'Yes, hello, I need information for medicine Iplex.'

The pharmacist paused. 'Iplex? I'll have a look on my computer.'

But he couldn't find it. Voula tried the next pharmacy, and the next. She crossed them off as she went. Some were helpful and gave her phone numbers to try. She wrote down all the information. She made phone calls until she heard Yiota's car in the driveway.

Voula and Tony were the only ones home. It was early afternoon. Tony was locked in the study talking on the phone. Voula was doing her puzzles. Tony's voice began to rise. She wheeled herself closer to the door.

'It's on your website that you're gonna provide Iplex to all named patients as part of the out of court agreement but it's been three months and nothing's happening ... The Australian government isn't standing in my way, I've found a doctor that can write me a prescription, now all I need is you guys to release Iplex ... Don't you dare say you understand ... My mother is sick and you have a drug that can save her ... Don't feed me shit that there's limited stock. Hire more people and make it ... It's all about driving up demand isn't it? So you can charge whatever you like when you release it ... this is all marketing for you ... lives for marketing ... No, I won't calm DOWN ...'

Voula wheeled herself back to the living room. When she heard Tony hang up, she resumed her own calls.

'I'm sorry, that drug isn't available in Australia,' the voice on the receiver said.

'But how I bring here?'

There was a clunk on the line. She quickly hung up.

The study door opened. Tony was crying.

'Mum, what are you doing?'

She pressed on the agonising pain in her chest. 'I—I want to help ...'

'I heard you on the phone. How long have you been doing this?'

A tear slid down Voula's cheek. 'A few months.'

Tony clasped his face, shook his head. 'Why is this so hard? Why, God, why?'

She tried to reach for him. 'It's alright ...'

Tony's hands dropped. 'It'll come soon, I promise. We've still got the Italian study ...'

'I know you are doing your best ...'

Tony's eyes came to rest on the coffee table where his keys were. 'I have to go.' He picked them up.

'Stay for dinner,' she said.

He couldn't look at her. 'I ... I can't.'

And he left.

They were toddler-sized pieces. That is how her food was prepared and eaten, along with sips of water. Her body was unlearning to swallow.

Each day it was a little harder to grip a pen for her puzzles, and then one day, she could not pick it up. She cried for a while and Teresa and Panagioti hugged her together. Tony joined in too. Voula asked Teresa to bring her the laptop. She wasn't sure what she wanted to type so she allowed her words to fall to her like tears:

Hope.

Coffin in your body.

Pancakes.

Two cups of flour.

Two and a half cups of milk.

She typed for weeks until she emptied her mind of her recipes.

When there were many people talking and she wanted to speak, nobody would realise because she was too quiet. When did simple tasks become so complicated? Like speaking, or having a shower, or turning over in bed, or picking up a glass of water? Sometimes she would sit and cry that tasks were so laborious, or that she couldn't remember a time when they were easy.

There were no futures left to dream about, goals, special trips. Sometimes she would try to believe, for a moment, that Iplex was almost here, just so she could taste motivation. But no matter how much she tried, she couldn't see herself better. She only saw bleakness, feeding tubes, a stationary body unable to do anything but think and blink. She hated the disease, what it had done to her. She did not want it to take all of her. She would not let it take all of her.

On her way to the bathroom with Panagioti one night, Voula saw Teresa and Tony at the computer. Teresa had fallen asleep on the desk but Tony was still clicking.

'Are we close?' Voula whispered.

His eyes were tired. 'Just hang in there. Soon.'

The air was thicker, breathing, just that little bit more difficult. She didn't tell anybody this. Days blurred and time confused her. Had an hour passed or a lifetime? There were many faces, people who loved her. Bright memories filled her mind, twelve years old helping her mother in the kitchen. Some days she would look at Teresa and forget, but then she would think of a white dress, Teresa's wedding day and never meeting her grandchildren. But then happier thoughts swept through, and she would forget again. And she wasn't sure if she was imagining, but her parents and brothers and sisters came to visit from Greece. They celebrated Christmas together. Her brothers played the bouzouki and sang old songs. Voula hummed the music in her mind.

One day we must all die, Voula thought to herself when the reality of the situation visited. We must follow the path to be with God. It is not the drug companies that control these things, it is God. Voula wanted so much to explain this to Tony, to help him understand, but there was no energy for such discussions.

'My light is slowly fading,' she whispered to Panagioti one night in bed.

He stroked her face. 'Don't give up.' But then she was asleep.

There were many words spoken around Voula. She was unsure who was saying them, or in what space and time they were taking place.

'Happy New Year, Mum! It's your year this year. This is the year we get Iplex!'

'Bring me the iron board,' Voula commanded, somewhere, to someone. 'I want to iron my husband's shirts. I am his wife, and I want to iron them.' And it was her frail arm, bony, skin draping, that slid the iron along the board that day, by some miracle, and it may have taken her half an hour to iron that shirt, but she bloody-well ironed it.

While she lay in bed, she overheard serious discussions, or maybe she was dreaming. 'It must be those new herbal pills she's taking ... yeah, she's strong ... she's got heaps of life in her ... she's just tired ...'

She asked for the priest. He came. She confessed her sins, received the Holy Communion. But then she had an idea. She wanted to pick cherries, just like she would in Greece when she was little. The family drove her to a farm a way away and she picked cherries, and ate them. Tony and Teresa hung cherries from their ears and they all laughed.

'Make a cherry flan for me,' Voula asked Teresa back at home.

The request instantly distressed her. 'I can't, Mama,' she said. 'Nobody can make the cherry flan like you.'

Voula took her hand. 'The recipe is on the computer. Make the flan with the cherries from the farm.'

Teresa nodded.

Teresa helped her mother to bed.

Voula heard Teresa making her cherry flan as she drifted.

6.

The Stones

When I brush my teeth at Mummy's house, with the electric toothbrush, I always turn around and look at the door. To make sure. I keep my eyes big to check, just in case, so I'm ready. When I have to spit the toothpaste, I turn quick to the sink, spit, then I turn to the door and look again to check there is nothing. Then I turn back to open the tap (it's a bit hard to open), drink the water (not drink drink, just rinse in my mouth and spit out), then I look at the door again just in case. I want Mummy to come with me but she won't. She's usually in the kitchen washing the dishes. Mummy is always washing dishes or working. It makes me sad. It's not like at Daddy's where he has Jane. It's just me and Mummy here. Sometimes I go to play at *Yiayia* and *Bapoo*'s house and my aunties come and it's so fun, but it's sad too because Mummy doesn't usually go when I go. If she goes there is lots of shouting about Mummy doing wrong things and I just go upstairs and play with my dolls.

'Mummy,' I call out, to check she's still there.

'Yeah?' she says from the kitchen.

'Nothing.'

I wash the electric toothbrush then I take off my yellow toothbrush and put Mummy's blue toothbrush on and put the toothbrush back on the charge. Now Mummy doesn't have to worry about putting her toothbrush back on.

I fill my water cup and take it to my room.

Mummy gets grumpy if I'm not in bed by 7:30 and it's almost 7:30. I find my pink eye mask, put it on my head, then get in bed. I don't know if I should tell her about the potion. Demet said not to say anything to anyone.

'Ready!' I call out.

'Coming,' Mummy says.

I get snuggly in my bed. I love my bed at Mummy's. It was her bed when she was little. Mummy comes in. 'All ready?'

'Yep.'

She sits on my bed. She sees my stones on my bed table. One white, one blue. 'Don't forget to take your stones to Daddy's house tomorrow. They'll give you strength. Remember what the lady said.'

I nod. Mummy tucks me in. She kisses my cheek one, two, three times. I love her kisses. They are the best.

After Mummy says goodnight and closes my light and goes to the other room, I stick my hand out, grab my stones, and bring them under the doona. I hold them so tight. I look around my room to make sure there is nothing coming from the wardrobe, especially Gs (I don't want to say the word in case I say it and they come but they are Mogwai first). Mummy doesn't like it that I saw the Gs movie at Daddy's house. She got really mad at him for showing them to me. The stones will protect me from Gs.

'You pick the stone that you're drawn to,' the lady at the shop said when Mummy and I went to the mountains. The shop had a nice smell and lots of curtains and crystals.

'She'd like one for courage and one for confidence,' Mummy said.

I chose two stones. I was worried it would be too much money for two but Mummy said it was okay. I hope she wasn't lying.

'We are going to be superheros!'

Demet is standing on the edge of the sandpit, and she's acting like a superhero. She's been saying it from the moment Mummy dropped me off at before-school care. I do want to be a superhero but she doesn't need to say it all the time.

'Did you make the potion?' I ask.

'I started yesterday. It's got glitter, glue, water, and a secret ingredient.'

'I'm going to be Healing Girl. So I can make people feel better, be less busy and have more money. What about you?'

'Listen Girl. So I can go around the school and help people listen to the teachings of Allah. You must believe in Allah, Rita, or you will go straight to hell. Do you believe?'

'Well I don't want to go to hell, so, yes I do.'

The bell rings. We start to make our way back to the line.

'I'm going to the toilet quickly,' Demet says, and she goes off.

I make it to the line. Someone taps me on the shoulder. I turn around. It's Anita.

'Why do you play with Demet?'

What a strange question to ask. 'Because I like to.'

'You shouldn't.'

'Why?'

'Because she's a Muslim, and Muslims are evil.'

No they're not. I don't say anything but I don't feel so good. I reach into my pocket for my stones. I squeeze them and think of what Mummy said.

'That's why she wears that scarf thing. I heard my Mum tell my Aunty Pippa.'

Demet comes out of nowhere and pokes me. I jump and laugh. Anita turns back around to her friends.

'We really need to make that potion soon,' I say.

'See, I told you! Everything will be better once we make it.'

I want Daddy to come home but Jane said he is going to be late tonight so she is going to put us to bed. It's a different world at Jane's house from the world at Mummy's house. I don't like that the worlds are so different, especially on the first day of the week.

'Rita is a sooky-la-la.' It's Derek. He won't leave me alone. Mummy said to ignore him if he teases me so that's what I'm going to do. I keep playing on my Switch. I think he's gone.

'Sooky, sooky!' He jumps up from behind the couch and I get a scare.

'Stop it!'

He hits me on the arm. Jane walks past with the washing basket.

'Derek hit me!' I tell her.

'Rita, don't be a dibadobber,' Jane says and keeps walking.

I go to my room and sit on my bed. I want Daddy to come home. I want to talk to Mummy and Daddy but I can't ask Jane. I put my hand in my pocket and get out my stones. I close my eyes and squeeze them.

'What are you doing?' Derek is at my door.

I wish we were allowed to close our doors. 'I have these stones and they are going to protect me against you. That's what my Mummy said.'

'What was *that*?' Jane hears from the other room. She comes in my room, stands next to Derek. 'What stones. Show me.'

I don't want to show her but I have to. I hold them out. 'Mummy got them for me.'

Jane laughs. 'What a load of rubbish. Give 'em here.' She takes them from my hand.

'They're mine,' I say, softly.

'Yeah? Well this is *my* house, and in this house we believe in God not stones.'

'My Mummy doesn't believe in God.'

She steps closer, taps into my forehead with her pointy finger. It hurts. 'Use your brain, Rita.'

Derek grins and walks away. Jane follows him.

'How was your day today, baby?' Mummy says on the phone. She just rang me and I'm in my pyjamas sitting on my bed.

'Okay.'

'Only okay?'

'Yeah.'

'Is everything okay?'

Nobody else is in my room but I don't know where Jane and Derek are.

'Yeah.'

'Are you sure? I want you to be able to tell me anything.'

'Yeah, I'm sure.'

'Well just squeeze your stones and think of what I told you. Nobody can hurt you with the stones. Okay?'

'Okay.'

I keep my eyes open until I hear Daddy come home late.

'The potion will be ready tomorrow,' Demet announces in the sand-pit again.

'You've been saying that all I week.'

'I know. But it's because some of the ingredients have been hard to find.'

I shake my head. 'I don't know about this. Glue? I am sure we are not meant to drink glue, even if it is in a potion. I better ask my mum.'

'I told you. It's magical! And the potion will lose its powers if any parents find out.'

I sigh.

'You do want me to still be your friend, Rita, don't you?'

'Yes, yes, I do.'

'And you still believe in Allah?'

'Yes.'

'Then don't tell anyone about the potion. Promise?'

She sticks her pinkie finger out to me. I hook my pinkie on. 'Promise.'

'And you promise to drink it when it's ready?'

I don't want to have no friends. Then who will play with me? 'Okay. Promise.'

It's so good to be back at Mummy's. I'm sitting on the couch watching TV. It's a show about mermaids. I wish I was a mermaid. That would be the best. I could dive under the water and meet all these different mermaids and go on adventures.

'Dinner's ready,' Mummy calls from the kitchen.

'Coming,' I say, but I want to finish this show first.

'Rita! Now, please.'

'Okay, okay.'

Mummy made my favourite, quiche. Yum. She cuts it up for me.

'So how's things, my love. How are the stones?'

'Good, good.'

'Did you bring them here?'

'Actually ... no ...'

'Well bring them next time.'

'I can't … really …'

She gets a confused face. 'Why?'

'Well, don't get mad, but Daddy and Jane said they are a load of rubbish and they took them away.'

'W hat!'

I knew it would happen. I don't want her to get mad at Daddy. But she already has her phone and is calling. Great. I don't even want the stones anymore.

'How dare you do that … That's right, send them back …' and she's yelling and shouting and all these things. She goes to the bedroom. I can still hear a few words. I don't understand some of the words. Custoby? Court? Maybe she means basketball court? She says Daddy won because has too much money. Won what? A game of basketball? By the time she hangs up the phone I'm not even hungry anymore. She comes back.

'He said he'll give them back to you. Just bring them here, okay? And don't worry about it.'

'Okay.'

She comes down on her knees, hugs me. 'I love you.'

I hug her back.

'Don't worry about it. Daddy said he was wrong to take the stones. He said he'll talk to you about it when you go over.'

'Well Jane took them, really.'

'Oh. It's okay. Don't worry about it.' She takes my hand. 'Look at me, please.'

So I look at her.

'I love you. I'm always going to look after you. I'm always going to protect you. In life, you got to stand up for yourself. You got to be brave. If something doesn't feel right, you got to say 'no', I don't agree'. Do you understand?'

'Yeah.'

'Good.'

'Mummy, can I stay with you more?'

She breathes deep, looks sad. She brushes the hair from my face. I like when Mummy does that. 'I'm trying. Can you try and tell your dad?'

I shake my head. Telling Dad is scary, he might tell Jane.

She nods. 'Okay. Eat your dinner and we'll play some UNO. I'm going to win this time.'

'No way! I will.'

We laugh. She tickles me. It's funny.

'Can we have some of my lollies from Scott's party last week?' I ask, excited. I raise my two eyebrows.

'Oh, about those ...'

'Mum! Did you eat them?'

'I told you to hide your lollies so I can't find them!'

I'm so upset. I'm going to cry. Really.

She goes in a panic. 'I'll buy you double what you had, tomorrow, Okay?'

My mum is so cute. She is really cute. I feel bad because she feels bad. 'Not double. Sugar is bad for you. It's okay. Maybe just ... three.'

'Okay, three! It's a deal. Shake on it.'

We shake hands. I need to find a better spot for my lollies.

She sits back on her chair and we eat a bit more quiche.

'Mum ...'

'Yeah?'

'I have to tell you something ... but don't get mad. Promise?'

'I won't.'

'It's about Demet ...'

7.

The Bookshop

I think about you coming into the bookshop.

It's the evenings that I'm drawn to, night owl that I am. I try to get there earlier but usually rock up about nine. They close at ten on weeknights, eleven on weekends. I don't know why my subconscious enjoys this kind of masochism, the unrealistic goals and ridiculous expectations, yet somehow these short windows of time make the magic happen. Down the back of the bookshop on one of the two red-leather armchairs near the staff-only entrance, my laptop and I sit together, synched like a pair of rumba dancers.

Having my stories published in the store newsletter is one of the perks of being resident writer. But this story is not appropriate at all. If you did come into the bookshop, I think you'd come in at night. Daytime does not suit your demeanour.

They are playing indie rock songs with seductive, tortured love lyrics that get your heart aching and longing for the magnetic, cataclysmic chemistry you once had with someone you knew wasn't good for you but you didn't care because it tasted so damn good. I absorb the music, it whirlwinds inside me then kicks words out via my fingers onto the page. Whether it's symphonies or drum thrash, I just need *something*. It adds to the excitement, not knowing which staff member's playlist will be running and where their music might carry me.

I don't know what I'd do if you came in.

I told you this is where I am on lonely nights so you know where to find me. If you did decide to drop in, it would be a haphazard decision. You'd be passing by after dinner at the Vegie Bar with friends, strolling down the opposite side of the road. As the Brunswick Street tram glides past and rings its bell, averting your attention to reveal the bookshop with its open and inviting door, you'll be reminded of me. The niggling guilt you have about me will tap you on the shoulder and you will have a choice, just like you did the night we met.

We met at Open Studio, that small bar in Northcote where the freaks of society congregate away from judgemental eyes and mingle with others who appreciate uniqueness. It was Spanish night and bands were playing one after the other, the mood was celebratory, summer fun and laughter smelling sweetly of sweat and tequila. The bar was at capacity both inside and out and bodies couldn't help but be pressed up against each other.

I was in the beer garden with friends. It was decorated in colourful hanging lights, and as soon as your beauty crossed my vision, I lost my breath. You were also chatting to friends. We exchanged a brief look and you smiled. I didn't hesitate. I went straight up to you.

'Hi, I'm Anna.'

You grinned and shook my hand. 'Simon.'

'I don't usually go up to people but you look really interesting.'

'You know, I was just about to come up to you too.'

We laughed at the familiarity of our meeting, as if it had also happened in lifetimes past. The conversation flowed. Placing your hand on the small of my back, you broke us away from the crowd, found us a little corner where we talked life's meanings. The chemistry had us double blinking. It radiated through the outdoor courtyard. Our friends looked upon us, amazed by the energy between us. Some moments don't conform to logic. We were one of those moments. You did not try to kiss me, you just listened, lowering my defences with your tainted eyes, you did not shy away from looking into my depths, it was as if I was already yours and you were already mine, like we could, without a second thought, run hand-in-hand into the questioning night and never return.

I wanted to kiss you. But then you were gone. I was looking for you, but you were nowhere to be found. Had I made you up? Were you even real?

I meet so many people and I am perplexed as to why our few hours together hang suspended in my mind. Did I feel what I felt, or did I want a moment like it so badly I imagined it?

In the bookshop, I'm typing away, using my words to complete my latest catharsis. Sometimes, when I'm trying to arrive at a line, I look up from my computer and daydream. What a shock it is to look up and find you there. I don't seem able to grasp my emotions. Am I hallucinating?

'Hey,' you say.

My instinct is to slap you across the face, yell. Why did you do that? Why did you put me through all that?

Instead I say, 'hey,' into your nervous eyes, their hazel amplified by your black and green checked shirt.

I place my laptop aside and stand. We stare at each other, completely still, and I'm thrown back into the disillusion of that night. The energy between us is just as strong, it swallows my anger. I've been telling myself that I'm never going to see you again, that I just need to accept it and move on. That some situations end with a question. But to see your face, your dark hair, you are the embodiment of everything I love and everything I despise about my Mediterranean roots. Your understanding of the expectations crushing you as a child, how they carry forward and affect your future, your personality, your interactions with others. I had sworn off Mediterranean men after my divorce. But experiencing you for those short few hours, I realised that only a Mediterranean man is capable of understanding all my facets. Not just any Mediterranean man, though. It has to be one who doesn't conform, who has broken out like me.

We watch each other, our vulnerabilities overflowing and exposed.

You hurt me, I want to say. In the same breath I want to say, hold me, kiss me, take me.

'What took you so long?' I half-joke.

You avert your gaze, take a breath, return to me. 'I'm sorry.'

I sigh. 'So here we are again then.'

You smirk. 'Yes, here we are.'

'I'll just put my computer behind the counter.'

I put it away and return to you. You go to speak then stop, like you're double-checking your thoughts, one of the delightful subtleties I noticed about you the night we met.

'How are you?'

'I'm …' I pause. 'I mean, I don't understand. You ask me to go for coffee across the road, tell me you'll be back in a minute, and then *leave*?'

'I know …' You reach for my shoulder, but I shrug before your hand can land. You lower it. 'I'm sorry. It just wasn't right. I just—it wasn't about you. I wasn't in a good place. I told you that night. I had a lot going on. I didn't want to drag you into it.'

Your response triggers my Mediterranean anger. 'Hey!' I start, but then a customer walks by and without thinking, I take your hand and pull you through the staff-only door to boxes and books in disarray. There is a kitchenette and a door that leads to a passageway separating the bookshop from the building behind.

'I tried to find you!' I hiss. 'The least you could have done was SMS me when I found your friend and passed on my number.'

You grab at my shoulders. 'I just … I couldn't! It was the right thing to do! For you!'

'You fuckwit, I don't need your protecting!'

We stop, gazes locked, fury on my end, surrender on yours. I abruptly bring my lips to yours, because I always make the first move, control freak that I am. You kiss me back with passion and fire. I hold your face and I don't care, I just want to disappear into you. Our arms tangle around each other, our kiss effortless, just like our exchange the night we met.

Later we slow, our lips part. I grin. 'There's a pathway just outside this door. It's narrow enough to fit two bodies.'

'I thought you were a good Greek girl.'

'I am.'

'So I was right. I said there was a naughty side to you and you insisted there wasn't.'

I grab you by the shirt, bring you to me, gently and nibble at your lips, then run the tip of my tongue underneath your upper lip. You whimper.

'Do you want to go outside or not?'

'Want.'

I reach for the doorknob behind me, pull you out into the arousing warm night—a tickle of a breeze—close the door behind us. The pathway is so narrow there's a wall behind us both. The moon illuminates enough. Your shy hands begin to trace my body, my shoulder, my arm. You drop a hand to my waist and we kiss softly, deliciously, just a tease of tongue, giggle at our silliness. We continue like this, at a steady pace, until your shyness recedes, and our laughter dissipates, you press me into the wall, our kiss grows ferocious, your hand reaches underneath my summer dress to my thigh, and now we are swimming into each other's intimate worlds. I've never done anything like this before. I can count on one hand the number of men I've slept with.

'Do you like that?' you ask, rubbing at my underwear. You kiss my neck. I'm yours.

'Yes … have you been thinking about doing this with me?'

'Doing what? This?' You venture underneath the cloth, slide two fingers into my wet warmth, and my hands scrummage for something to hold on to because I'm spinning. My hands dive underneath the back of your shirt, I grab at your flesh, the muscular strength of you, quiver, moan, my need for more of you undeniable.

'Fuck me now.'

'No. What's the rush?'

I squeeze your forearms. 'I want it now.'

Before too long you are making your way inside me.

You're thrusting, pushing deeper, breathless, alive.

I take hold of your face, force you to look into my eyes. 'Why did you do it?'

You close your eyes, suck on my ear lobe, kiss my neck. I feel so invincible with you moving inside me, but I'm searching for answers, I want truths, in this moment I want and I want and I want.

'Answer me.'

'I told you.'

You rub my clit and I'm reaching for the wall behind you, to grab something, safety, clarity. I kiss your neck, bite into it, but you're unperturbed. 'You just wanted to fuck me, didn't you?'

You're losing control now. 'What are you talking about?'

'You wanted a fuck and when you realised I was a single mum you aborted, walked away. I'm right, aren't I?'

We're getting uncontrollably louder and I'm worried about people hearing us but I'm not giving up, it's important I know now, I have to know now. 'Answer!'

You stop, look into my eyes. You kiss my lips sensually. You're still moving inside me but you've slowed now, you're going so slow, teasing, weakening me, assuming your control, each thrust further eroding my defences, compounding my need for pleasurable relief.

'Answer ...'

'Well ... What difference does it make? I'm fucking you now aren't I?'

'But this isn't real. This is a story.'

'Whether I'm fucking you in reality or I'm fucking you on the page, I'm still fucking you.'

You seal our deal with a gentle, passionate kiss, like the kiss of death. Slide your hand over my mouth. You increase your speed, claim my body, and once again we don't make sense, and it's with this known unknown that we both continue our ascent, climb the mountain of our uncertainty, higher and higher and higher, come, come, come, *explode* into the Fitzroy night.

I think about you coming into the bookshop. Not sure what I'd do if you ever did.

8.

Theo and Haroula

Theo

The best moment of every day is when I unlock the front door of my house. This is what it's all about; the sound of the patter and thud of my four boys running toward me with their massive grins, calling out 'Daddy! Daddy!', mauling me, jumping on me, hanging off me, swinging off me. And even though my back hurts and my head aches from dealing with all the *malakes* down at the factory, I love it. My Mrs, she just stands with her hands on her hips, but she's happy I'm home too.

I'm a lucky man, I know I'm lucky, but I've worked hard for that luck. I live in my dream suburb, Ivanhoe, I have a nice corner block with a big house. When I want something, ninety-nine percent of the time I can get it. Flat screen TVs, I got one in the living room, one in my bedroom, and one outside in the bbq-outdoor area near the pool. Nike runners, Armani aftershave, Ralf Lauren polo shirts—I even got matching ones for me and my boys. We're the five stooges me and my boys. I can't say no to them. Whatever they want, they get. They want ice-cream, they get ice-cream. They want to go to the zoo? We're going to the zoo. They want to sleep in our bed? Join the party.

I don't want to see my boys cry—ever. Crying is for girls and poofs. No boy of mine is crying. And no boy of mine is being gay. That's why I make sure I toughen them up with some play fighting, point out a beautiful chick or a nice rack when one happens to cross my path, digitally or in real life. My boys are going to grow up to be champions of the world.

My Mrs, Anthea, she's the best wife a man could ask for. We met at Venue, the Greek night at Billboards nightclub on Russell Street, in the 90s. One of my mates was trying to pick up one of her friends and our groups mingled. We were both young, studying business at Latrobe Uni. I remember thinking she seemed really soft when I started talking to her. I liked that. It's funny the stuff you remember because even though it was so long ago, I remember the song 'To Dilitirio' was playing, and we were cracking a joke about it being so full on and how Greeks are so dramatic with their suicide tunes. Straight away we started hanging out and the rest is history.

Anthea stays home, looks after the kids—no boy of mine is going to childcare. She cooks the best foods, keeps the house clean. I don't even mind mess but she keeps everything shiny and in its place, as best as she can of course—my house is like a toy shop. I get each of my boys a small present every week. We got a room upstairs full of toys. I buy my Mrs gifts too, at least once a month, usually with roses. Not those piss-weak ones that flop when you touch them, I mean long-stem, strong, red roses. I like to mix it up with pink and orange sometimes. Only the best for my wife. She has a credit card with no limit, and every Friday I give her $1,000 in cash to have in her purse. We got a cleaner come in once a fortnight too.

I don't really believe in all that stuff about there being one person on the planet for all of us. I hate romantic shit and I don't ever kiss Anthea in front of anyone—that's my own private business. But if I did, say, believe in that shit, then Anthea would have to be my person, my soul-mate. But like I said, I don't like talking about emotional stuff. Anthea's like that too, which is why we are a perfect match, me and my Anthea. Yeah we got married young, and our life has just become about work, kids, home, but I'd rather be with Anthea than without. Theo and Anthea forever.

We built our house close to the business, but on some days I think the swimming pool is too small and that I'd like a twenty-seater theatre room instead of the ten seater. Everything I own, one day, it's all going to my boys. My job will be done when I know my boys will be taken care of when I'm gone. That's what success is for me. That's why I work like a *mavro,* a black man. And I don't mean leaving them like a hundred grand each. Nah, I mean I want them to have at least two houses each (one investment property and one to live in), plus at least a mil in the bank. Of course they'll also get their share of the business. It'll have to be split between me and my sister first though. I don't know why she gets half when she doesn't contribute not even a quarter of what I do. But that's what Dad said and so that's what's happening.

My dad is my idol, my hero. He came to this country with ten bucks in his pocket and now he's got a million-dollar business. The Aussies treated him like crap, called him a dumb wog, but it's funny who came up dumb in the end. He told me stories. When he started the dip stand at South Melbourne market, they all thought it was the stupidest idea selling *tarama* and *tzatziki* my mum made. But now where are all those dumb cunt Aussies? They're probably all still drinking beer at the pub and working at the market. Not one of them can say they got their dips and yoghurts in Coles and Woolies and supermarkets around Australia and New Zealand. And you know why? Because they think they're so good but they're not. They're the stupidest *ratsa* (race) in the world. That's what I want to say to them when I go to conferences and industry meetings and they look at me like I'm the wog that came to their country and took all their business—I was born here, you idiot. If your race is lazy, that's your problem, not mine. And I'll crack their footy jokes and their booze jokes to get on their level and talk business, and we'll all act like we're best buddies, but deep down I know what they think. They think I'm a dirty fucking wog.

Don't get me wrong, I'm a good guy—I've helped heaps of people out with money and stuff. I have to deal with all sorts of different races for my business, like the *Indiani*, don't get me started on them. Another lazy race. But when it comes to the Aussies, I won't forget. I forgive them for what they did to my dad but I will never, never forget. And if any of them, or any other *malaka* crosses me, I got connections to bikie gangs and all sorts of people who got my back. And there have been times I've needed to use those connections, and I never felt bad after, not for a second. Because if you cross me, or my family, you'll pay. It's that simple.

Sometimes, when work's really busy, I'll admit I get frustrated. Maybe it would have been nice if I was given a choice. But I knew, since I could comprehend stuff, maybe from two years old, that I'd be taking over the business. My dad would tell me every day. He'd come home from work and he'd say 'I will show those *Afstrali* who I am. I will build my business and I will show them and one day, Theo, one day, you will sit at the top. I am working hard for you.' I got a really sharp memory. My mind is like an axe. Nothing gets past me. I remember how tired Dad was coming home from the market. I remember him in the kitchen with my mum, with big bowls and yogurt and *tarama* everywhere, trying to get the dips just right. They'd always get me and my sister to have a taste. We've been part of the business since the day we were born.

But yeah, sometimes, when I'm really fucking tired and a distributor's rubbed me the wrong way, or an employee has pissed me off because a fucking *Indiano* wants extra pay he doesn't deserve, yeah on those days I wish I didn't have the business. At night, when I try and sleep, I feel like the business—like the actual business—is sitting on my chest, crushing me down, and I swear to God sometimes I feel like it's crushing me into the earth. On those nights, I sort of wish I had a life of my own. I even thought once, that I could be a politician. I know, it sounds dumb, but I'm pretty good with talking and expressing myself. I got top marks in high school and uni. Dad's always been proud of me. Never had any complaints with me. He always tells me I'm the best son. Now Dad's getting old, pulling away from the business, and so he should, he's worked hard. He's always helped me and my sister with anything we need. He even gave me and Anthea a house for our wedding present. Tell me a dad who would do that?

I've just come home from my work and my in-laws are over. They come down once a week to help Anthea with the boys. As the boys hang off me, they greet me.

'Hey,' I say to Anthea. So fucking good to see my lady.

'Mum made roast chicken.' Anthea's setting the table.

'Perfect. Thank you,' I say to my mother-in-law. I don't call her by her name. I don't call her anything. I know it's customary to call your in-laws Mum and Dad, but I explained to them years ago, before I married Anthea, that I feel like I'm disrespecting my parents if I call them Mum and Dad. I'm lucky they understood. I've been pretty lucky with my in-laws.

I sit on the couch with my boys.

TThen I hear the front door open and I think for a minute 'who could that be now?' Dad didn't say he was coming over and neither did my sis, but it's Mum, and she's holding an oven dish. What's she doing now? Fuck. What's going on now?

'Haroula, how are you?' my mother-in-law says in Greek.

'Good, good,' Mum says in Greek. 'I didn't realise you were here. I cooked stuffed peppers.'

'Mum, I told you yesterday they were coming. Don't you remember?' I say in Greek.

She lowers her head. 'Sorry, Theo. I try to help.'

'Yeah, always trying to help but not helping,' I mutter under my breath. Only Anthea hears and understands, because she gives me a look not to push it any further. Maybe I shouldn't have said that. Now I feel bad.

'It's okay, Mum,' Anthea says, taking the dish from Mum. 'More for us to eat.'

'But Theo does not eat leftovers. Who will eat the food?'

'It's okay, *simbethera*,' my mother-in-law says to Mum. 'You will take some for tomorrow and I will take some and all will be okay.'

Nobody goes beyond this point and we all sit at the table to eat.

'Come and eat, Haroula,' my father-in-law says, but Mum's just sitting on the couch looking awkward. I honestly wish she would just go.

'No, it is okay, I'll go,' she says. But she stays.

After we eat, I go to my bedroom and call Dad.

'Yeah, she's here. Can you come get her? I've got my in-laws over.'

It's a good thing my parents live just down the road. Dad comes and gets her pretty quickly, gently. Like I said, Dad is my hero.

Haroula

I am in the bed again. I feel like one life I been laying in a bed. When I lay here sometimes I think why I come to this ugly place. Ugly country. Cold place. No sunshine. I like it in my village in Cyprus. Everything is close, and then if I want to go to the city, I catch the bus. Here in this country, all the roads and places are too far. There is too much space and you can't breathe. You breathe the cold into your lungs and your whole body and soul it becomes cold. And the people, the Australians, they are such cold people. The country and the people—cold. That is why my husband take me home once a year to our place, Cyprus. Our home. I'm so happy when I go. I never stay in bed there. If I do not go home once a year they will find me dead on this bed.

This country is the worse place I been to in my life. I did go to other places in Europe with my husband a little bit but mostly I just want to be home. I really think I would have a good life in Cyprus if I stay. All my brothers, okay so they do not have much money as us, with the economy crisis now, but at least they have home. You can't replace home with a fake home. Home is home.

All my sisters we had to leave, we had no choice. Things were not easy in my country. I remember when I was a young, I think seven years about, everyone celebrate in the street after the *Enklezi* leave and Cyprus is its own country. Most of the country want to join with our motherland but there was too much trouble to join Greece so they make us our own country. But I hear my father say the papers the politicians sign were not good: the *Enklezi* army would stay in Cyprus forever; Turkey, Greece and the *Enklezi* to keep the island peaceful. But what is peace? That is what my father would say. Anytime someone cough they could come and take our island.

My father was right. Fourteen years later, the Turkish come with their men and their guns. We have to leave my village near Kyrenia with only the clothes on our back. I see the dead bodies in the street. I hear the gun shots. Women shrill, I never forget. My friend Nuvit who live three houses away in my village, I never see her or her family again. All the Turkish-Cypriots had to stay in the north, and all the Greek-Cypriots, they force us to leave to the south of the island, same with the Turkish-Cypriots in the south, they make them go to the north. In the middle of the night we went to the other side of the island to stay with my *thio* and his family, and there was no room, ten in one small room.

We had to find a new home there. But there was not even enough money to eat. One chicken for fifteen people, and only on a Sunday. My father sent me to Australia to marry my husband with only a photo. There was no money for a *brika* to marry. He would say it was the *Enklezi* that destroy Cyprus, and the Americans, they all want our island because of where it is. The *Enklezi* took the land of the Aborigines in Australia too. *Enklezi* and Australians, cold, cold people. I never go back to my house in Kyrenia, even after they opened the Green Line and you could go with the passport. But in my dreams it sometimes comes, and I think of the blue sea and of my friends playing in the streets of the village.

Ever since I come to this country I been in bed. From nineteen years old. I arrive on the ship at Princess Pier, my *thio's* friend he ready to take me to meet my husband. It was very quick the marriage. I always like to be marry and dress in the white. Maybe one month after I come I be married. My husband bring me to a small flat in South Melbourne and I just go into the bed and I never want to come out. It's like the bed is a coffin for me. I been dead for thirty-five years. The only time I come out is to cook for my family, and of course, for the dips—I love the dips.

Sometimes when I am in the bed, my mum is lying next to me and she sings me songs. There were nine of us children and my dad, we were all very scared of him. I never look him in the eyes. My mum, they all think in the village that she is crazy but I know my mum was not crazy, she was just tired. But a friend of mine she tell me she heard my mum try to jump from the cliff. I do not know if this is true or a story they told my mum to get her to go in the crazy person home but they took her anyway. I remember when they take her, the men, the scary men with nothing on their faces, they say to her 'you coming with us, you need to come with us' and she yell, no, she shrill, very loud, that the entire village hear her, she say 'I want death, I want death. I belong to death.'

What we do, all of us children, we take care of each other. Many months later she come back. I remember when I go on the ship to Australia and my mum she crying and crying and I was crying and crying and I remember when the ship was sailing away, I remember, I never forget, I remember I could hear her screaming 'my daughter, my daughter', and I wish in that moment I could hold her but I could not hold her, I had to just stand on the ship and cry all alone because I could not reach my mum and I did not know where I was going, if I would see her again, if I would ever come back.

When my mum lie next to me sometimes in my bed, she tell me she misses me and she holds me.

The door opens. It is my husband. 'You have your appointment with Ilia in two hours. Theo will take you. Come, rise.'

'No, I don't want to go.'

'You need to. Come, I will help you.' My husband come to my bed and help me up. He help me dress and wash my face. He give me a sandwich because lately I too dizzy to even cook. I make those *yemista* the other day for Theo but before that I no remember the last time I cook and I no cook since the *yemista*. I do not know how many days it been since the *yemista*. My husband give me my pills to take.

T*heo*

Anthea calls me pencil bum because I got a new bike and I wear bike shorts. You got to wear the shorts if you don't want your bum to hurt. My bike cost me $5,000. It's so light I can fly from the factory to my place in under twenty minutes. And it keeps me fit and trim.

I ride in from work and take the BMW to Mum's. She's ready to go when I get there. I give her a hug. 'How are you today?' I ask her in Greek.

She shrugs.

We drive to Mum's doctor, and while I'm driving, I think about the doctor (he's Greek). You know, I always trust the Greeks above all races. If a guy is Greek, he's my brother. But a few days ago, one of my best mates, Sam, came over after my boys flaked it on my bed, and seriously, I never seen him so upset. I sat him down and got him a scotch, and I knew what it was about. His sister was due to go to court for mediation over custody of her kids and the asset split of the divorce. It didn't go well.

'She had no chance of winning, man. It's the lawyers. They were egging her on from the start, telling her she was gonna win, telling her to trust them because "we're like family because we're Greek". But she had no chance, Theo. No chance, man. Her ex has too much money. He played so dirty. She should have settled a year ago.'

I couldn't believe what he was saying. 'But you did your research before you told her to go to them. I remember you said they were clean when you Googled.'

'Google? They're lawyers!' He shook his head. 'I'm so *dumb*. Lawyers can be Google free because they can sue for defamation if you write something bad about them. And it's up to the person accusing to prove what they are saying is true. It's not like America where it's the other way around. And they're lawyers! Like you could stand a chance going up against a lawyer. They made all their stupid promises verbally, not in writing.'

I shook my head. 'Oh my God, what shifty cunts.'

'Theo, we got fucked up the arse, big time. Fucked up the arse by Greek lawyers.'

I didn't know what to say, how I could help. I was trying to stay focused on Sam but all I could think about was how Mum's doctor is Greek.

But also, my family's not Greek, we're Cypriot, and it's not exactly the same thing, although a lot of Greeks and Cypriots don't like it when you say that but they can go to hell. Like you can't deny that sometimes the Greeks think they're better than us, like they're the superior race and we're just the islanders. I mean, did they *really* want *enosis* with us before the war? Would they *really* have taken us in when we had a small Turkish-Cypriot population? But of course, better Greeks than non-Greeks. Cyprus is small, we need to stick together in Australia, which is why most of my mates, including Sam, are Greek.

Still, if I ever had my days as a politician, I would want the people of Australia to know that while we have similarities we are not part of Greece, we are our own country, with our own language (similar to Greek but not exactly the same), our own flag, still with British military bases on our land (they need to fuck off), still with Turkey illegally occupying the top half (they also need to fuck off). And they think we don't notice them importing mainland Turks to increase their numbers and negotiating power – Turkish-Cypriots are a minority over there now – what a joke! And the whole world pretends like it's not happening and we're just some exotic holiday destination. Most people in Australia wouldn't even know the difference between Greece and Cyprus, they just think we're all the same thing, which bloody pisses me off big time. My grandfather told me all this stuff when I went to Cyprus on my honeymoon, how Cyprus is still a prisoner to the English, and how they set it all up, that's how I know.

If you look at the facts, this Greek doctor has made a mint off us the last fifteen years. Mum's been getting by, but these last months he changed her pills and Mum's lost it. She can't even cook or remember what day it is.

When we get to the doctors, we take a seat, and the receptionist asks if we want something to drink, in Greek.

'I'll have a latte,' I say.

'Water for me, please,' Mum says in Greek.

Before the drinks come Dr Papathanasiou comes out and I stand.

'Hey, Theo,' he says, shaking my hand, patting me on the forearm.

'Hey,' I say shaking his hand, pretending everything's normal.

'*Perase*, Haroula,' he says, ushering my mum.

'Actually, I'd really like to see you on my own first, if that's okay.'

He stops. 'Sure, Sure. Mary,' he gestures to the receptionist, 'bring Theo's coffee in when it's ready.'

'Here it is,' she chimes, coming from the kitchen.

I take it, say thank you. I give mum a kiss and then Dr Papathanasiou and I head into his room.

He has two arm chairs in the small room, a coffee table between them. I sit opposite him. He's got lots of art in his rooms. I never noticed it before but now I'm wondering how much it all cost.

'How's the business, Theo? All going well?'

'Yeah. We're branching out into crackers so it's exciting times.'

'You know I always get Nick's dips when I go to the supermarket.'

'Well they're the best.' I smile.

'Of course! What can I do for you?'

'I just wanted to talk about Mum. She's not herself lately.'

'Yes, you mentioned on the phone last week …'

'I'm just worried. Actually, I'm more curious why you changed her pills.'

He coughs. 'Well I didn't feel she was responding to her previous medication, and this new drug's just come out on the market, lots of research has gone into it, it has less reported side-effects—'

'It also costs $1000 a month.'

'Yes. It's one of the best. I always recommend the best to my clients.'

I take a sip of my latte. 'I been thinking I'd like Mum to go and see another doctor.'

He laughs. 'You're pulling my leg, aren't you *re malaka*?'

'Nah, man, I'm not.' I sip my latte in his panicked silence. 'Look, I'm not happy. Mum's not well and I want another opinion. She was in hospital again only a month ago and they recommended to us when we went to the Epworth that we should get another opinion.'

'Theo, Theo,' he says, like he's trying to deflate my suspicions, 'don't listen to the Aussie *malakes* down at the Epworth. They just want your money. Your mum knows me. If you pull her now who knows what it's going to do to her. She has a relationship with me. We've built trust.'

'I respect that, but I've made up my mind. I want her file.'

He clears his throat. 'Look, I wish I could help you, but I can't just release her file to you. It needs to be her next-of-kin which is your dad.'

I rise from my chair. 'I knew you were a fucking shifty cunt.'

'Now, Theo, there's no need for accusations.'

'Give me her fucking file!'

'I'm sorry, I can't.'

Fucking cunt. I try to breathe but all I can feel is all the family responsibilities and problems crushing down onto my chest. I go out and tell Mum that we're leaving, but she says she wants to see the doctor.

Haroula

Theo say that I no have to see Ilia again, that I go to another doctor at the Epworth hospital. But it is rude of me to not have one more session with him since I be here. I need to say goodbye to him. Theo tell me he wait outside while I talk to Ilia.

Ilia ask me if I am okay and I say I sleep more lately. I tell him that my mum she sleeping next to me all the time. He writes on his papers.

'What does your mum say?' he asks me in Greek.

'She says she wants me to go to her, to return to Cyprus.'

'It is common to miss people that we have lost and imagine them in our sleep.'

'But my mum is in Cyprus. I have not lost my mum.'

Ilia not say anything. He look at me funny, like I no know what I say. My head start to hurt again and I need a bed. I need my bed. I tell him I need my bed.

'Your mum died when you were twenty-five, Haroula.'

I stand up from my chair. 'Why would you say such a horrible thing to me? Why would you curse my mother like this?'

And then Theo, he come inside the room, and I screaming, I'm crying, and he is talking to Ilias and the nurse is coming in, and they say they are going to take me to the hospital again. I'm going to go to the hospital and Theo he is mad, he is very mad at Ilias, but Theo he take me out of the room and back to the car.

'It's okay, Mother,' Theo say to me in Greek. He look scared. 'I'm going to look after you. You're going to be okay.'

'Where is my mum?'

'Why are you asking about Grandmother, Mum?'

'Is my mum dead?'

'Yes, Mum, why would you think she is not dead?'

'Where are you taking me, Theo?'

'To the hospital, Mum. You will be better. I promise.'

But then I see her while we drive, I see my mum. Theo is talking on the mobile phone. We are stop at the traffic lights and I see my mum walking on Doncaster Road between the cars. She call me to come. She call me to come. Mum! Mum! My Mum! I go to go to my mum. I be back before Theo knows that I am gone. I open the door and run to her.

9.

The Mother Must Die

I should just die. I may as well. It may be a week, a month, two years, ten years, but I will die. I will be buried, stuffed in a coffin and the maggots will eat me. They will. Fuck it. If I'm going to die, then I should just die. The world is fucked. We're all doomed.

Take this office space—open plan, open, robots punching at their computers, blocking the reality of death.

Gary stops at my desk, presents a fake smile. 'You'll get that report done by Friday?'

'Sure, Gary,' I reply.

'Great stuff.'

He walks away. He made me redundant last week. Swept away the unreliable part-time mother of the organisation, put her out with the trash. Fuck you, Gary. You think you're some big-shot manager in an expensive suit. You're a nobody, a speck on this melting planet. You could cross the road tomorrow morning and be flattened.

So, fuck you. Ha.

'Should I just die?' I ask my fat supervisor while she explains what I need to get done by my last day.

She sort of chuckles, her double chin wobbles. 'Die?' she asks in her Pommy accent. 'What do you mean?'

But I'm not laughing. I'm not even frowning. I just sit there, opposite her, at the round table in her office on the thirty-seventh floor of this important corporate building.

I stare into her. 'Just die. Like, catch the lift to the highest floor and jump off this mother fucking building. What do you think?'

She lowers her gaze, clears her throat, and it sounds phlegmy, a thick putrid substance of bother, or guilt, or something. 'Do you think you need to speak to someone?' Her voice is low. 'It could be postnatal depression. I can relate. I'm a mother too.'

Maybe I should push her off the building. I'd kind of like to see her round body burst like a water balloon. I raise my eyebrows at her. 'It's a bit late for postnatal depression—my daughter is three. And how can you relate? You've been taking your son to childcare five days a week since he was six weeks old.'

She doesn't seem like she knows what to do with me; doesn't seem like she needs this kind of issue right now. I stare out the window. A helicopter is flying in the sky. I want it to smash in sideways and mangle us both into the office furniture. She slides her chair out, leaves the room. I try to calculate how far up I have to go for my body to splatter.

A hand comes to rest on my shoulder, zaps me out of the calculation. I know it's him.

'Take me home,' I say, from somewhere. And zombie-like he leads me out of the office, into the lift, and down, down, down, until my ears are blocking.

He drives us towards suburbia. Soon the scary buildings are behind us. Local shops blur but then come into view. I begin to breathe.

'Do you want to talk about it?'

I shake my head.

'What happened?'

'Life happened.'

He pats my thigh. 'It's going to be okay.'

'I hate everyone.'

'A business can't function on someone working two days a week.'

'I want to be with Nadia.'

'That's just the way the world works.'

'I'm a mother.'

'You can't be both.'

'Then why was I told I could be both?'

'Who told you that?'

I stare out my window, but I'm waiting for it. I'm waiting.

'Have you been taking your pills?'

I don't respond. Cars fly by. Life is zapping by. How do you catch it? How do you hold it in your hands?

'That's why this is happening,' he finally says.

'Of course.'

'We have a child. You can't be … emotional around her. It's not good for her.'

'Yes.'

'You need to stay on the pills.'

'Yes.'

'It's what's best.'

'Is that why we haven't fucked for the last year too?'

There. I've said it now. *There.* The words unfurl my neatly-packaged world. I start to cry thick tears. They run down my face fast. Life is a glacier I've been frozen into. I am an exhibition. Tour buses can drive by on excursions and point: *there is woman; there is mother, faceless, frozen by her anguish.*

The car has stopped. We've arrived at the childcare centre. I wipe my face.

Outside an icy wind penetrates my bones. I pull my jacket tight around my waist. He embraces me. I let him. In his touch there is nothing, and I am nothing. This is how it is, how it will always be. Yet inside me, emotions run like wild horses. I yearn to mount them and ride to the centre of the earth where tribal women congregate. I want to dance under the moonlight; howl and chant, with my body naked and free I want to sing *I am woman, I am mother, I am woman, I am mother.*

He types the security code on the door keypad. The doors open and we walk towards her room. The hallway walls are covered in drawings and parenting advice. We stop at her door. The room's activity journal sits open on a lectern. My fingers gently caress the clear plastic page. I can feel him behind me reading. There's a photo of Nadia and two other boys. The long description underneath reads:

We played in the trickle stream. Observed by Tina Rice on the 22nd of July 2009

Brian, Nadia and Josh wanted to play in the trickle stream. It was so hot. They held hands and walked through the garden to the stream.

Brian sat on the grass and started taking his socks off. 'No sockies,' he said.

Nadia giggled and pointed at the stream. 'Water,' she said. She plonked herself on the grass and started taking her shoes and socks off.

Brian threw off his hat. Tina, the carer, saw. 'Brian, we have to wear our hat in the sun. Could you please put on your hat?'

'No hat,' Brian said.

Nadia, who had successfully taken her shoes and socks off, stood up. She picked up Brian's hat. 'You wear hat, Brian,' she instructed, approaching him. She put the hat back on Brian's head. He didn't object.

Josh was already barefoot. He crouched to the grass and put one foot into the pond. He looked up at Nadia. 'Play rocks?'

Nadia moved to the edge of the pond and picked up a small rock. She examined it. 'Pretty rock. Nice rock.' She looked over at Brian who was stepping into the pond. 'Throw rock?' she asked him.

Brian didn't respond. He was busy placing his fingers under the trickle stream. Nadia threw the rock into the pond. This got their attention. The boys laughed.

'Splash,' they both said.

'More splash,' Nadia agreed.

They splashed in the pond until it was time for lunch.

Nadia's grinning in the photo. I look up through the tinted glass window and into the room. She is sitting at a small table in the corner kneading dough. There is a little boy opposite her and they are chatting. Nadia handles the dough like it's one of the most interesting and pleasurable things in the world.

Her cheeks are round like mine. I ache to kiss them, to inhale her soft, innocent scent. But I can't. I can't reach. My child. I don't know why. I don't know what's happening to me. My child that I birthed, that came out of me. My *child* that is me.

He enters the room. Her face brightens when she looks up and sees him. Her smile deepens the dimples. She runs towards him. He picks her up, kisses her. They chat. She's looking around. Her mouth shapes around the letters 'Mummy? Mummy?' She's looking around but can't find me. I stare at her through the glass, my breath quickening to the pace of her anxiety. 'Mummy? Mummy?' She can't see me. The glass is one-sided. I touch the glass with my fingers, caress their image. I imagine that I am him. That I'm the one holding her, smiling into her eyes. I imagine Nadia as an adult, looking into my eyes, touching my face. I imagine her as a woman. *I'm proud of you, Mum.*

The horses run faster ...

10.

Smelly Francesco

Francesco stank. There was never a day that he did not. His stench was a bitter mix of garbage and stale breath, cigarette smoke and plaque. The grotesque odour coated every cell of his skin. He was beyond redemption. The stench had even woven its way into the fibres of his worn-out clothes. All the attire he had to his name was stuffed into a wardrobe that leaned to one side in his tiny, one bedroom flat within the tower housing commission flats in Reservoir.

Francesco contributed nothing to society. He was a pathetic, sixty-one-year-old balding man who sucked government support and the tax-payer dollar. It had been ten years since he had worked at the mechanic shop; fifteen years since he lived with anyone, if you didn't count Esmeralda. Francesco was an oxygen thief, an insult to human existence. Nobody usually cared enough to call him a friend, or family, or anything. And when they did, it was because they had their own agenda.

His activities were much the same from day to day. The morning walks to the local milk bar for the *Herald Sun* and packet of Peter Stuyvesant. The Asian lady who owned the store was always nervous around him. This amused Francesco. He would flash the golden tooth within his crooked smile, his gaze violating and perverted. He took pleasure in watching her cringe.

After the walk, nothing much—maybe some television, a *Days of Our Lives* episode, the release of toxic gases. Sometimes Esmeralda would come by. If Francesco pushed enough there would be vulgar sex and grunting. But Esmeralda's mind was always on the gambling. Most nights Francesco would attend the poker game at Luigi's with Esmeralda by his side, encouraging him to raise the stakes.

Francesco owed a lot of money to the wrong people. For a long time, he had dealings with the wrong people.

Wherever life blew Francesco, on weekdays he would always be home at three in the afternoon, hoping for some word, some communication, some hope of reconciliation. Standing by the rectangular mailboxes at the front of the flats, smoking and waiting. His eyes would scan the quiet street nobody dared to walk down, anticipating the appearance of a fluorescent orange saint on a motorcycle: the postman.

There was mail on some days. But it was always bills. Just bills.

Francesco was a restless sleeper. Five hours a night was a success for him. Perhaps it had something to do with the Melbourne winters he simply could not adapt to, even after so many decades in Australia. The apartment walls were thin, and it was too expensive to have the heater running all the time. When the blaring red numbers on his bedside clock ticked over to single digits deep in the pitch of the night, and he was still not asleep, his heart raced. He could feel the shadow of death in his room, its gaze penetrating him, judging him for his past, and he would hold himself tight to eradicate the sensation of death's pointy fingernails running over his skin. On those nights, as a precaution, he would take an extra tablet of his heart medication. He would close his eyes and force his mind to take him to places of warmth, even though he did not deserve to visit such places.

He would think of home and his older brother, Dante, how they would slurp swirls of homemade spaghetti tossed in organic tomatoes and basil, hand-picked from the fields of Signior Ruberto. Their legs once dangled from their chairs as they raced down their meals and when the last strand was devoured, they would tear into the promising afternoon, the familiar rays of the Tuscan sun warming their faces. Francesco kept his vision firm on Dante as they sprinted through narrow, pebble-stoned streets, Francesco eager to outrun Dante to the village shops, to prove that he was just as athletic, just as much a man as Dante was. But he never won …

On sleepless winter nights, when the cold froze his bones, the craving for familiarity was essential to keep breathing, Francesco thought of the family he had created, the one he had not seen in fifteen years. He did his best to block out the fights with his ex-wife, the tear-stained faces of his children. Instead he thought of family trips to the Great Ocean Road, dinners at the Pancake Parlour at Northlands, sweltering summer days at the Coburg pool, and his inability to be firm, always caving in to his children's every desire.

And on those nights, when the family haunted his mind, the sobs would tear from his soul; tortured, deep, inconsolable, escaping through the cracks in the walls and echoing through the run-down flats he deservingly called home.

Francesco fumbled with his tie. It had been years since he had knotted one. And the brown, fifteen-year-old tweed suit! It was more like a practical joke than a piece of formal attire. When he had retrieved it from his wardrobe two days ago, the dust had been thick enough to scrape. He hung it by the coat hanger on the curtain rail and opened the window to air it. But the icy winter rain had blown, turning the dust into some sort of mud. At this point, he probably should have surrendered to the gods and collapsed on the sofa, but instead he wet a cloth and wiped down the suit. It was insanity. He shouldn't have been going. He had no plan, no rehearsed speech. What in God's name was he going to say?

There was a slight tremor in Francesco's hands as he pulled on his tie. If only he had a mirror to examine his ridiculousness. Maybe then he would have reconsidered. He wiped the sweat forming on his brow.

A sudden knock at the door startled him. Esmeralda. He heard the keys and then the door burst open. Francesco briefly looked up then returned to brushing his suit sleeves. Esmeralda placed the keys on the kitchen bench, stood with her hands on her hips, her jet black hair draping down her back.

'What you doing, Francesco?' she said in her illustrious, Spanish accent.

He scratched his freshly shaven face. 'I go somewhere tonight.'

A high-pitched laugh yodelled from her. 'Where you go, you silly man?' she said, bunching three, red-manicured fingers and shaking them at him. 'You look ridiculous in that suit. Luigi and the others will laugh at you.'

'I no go to the game tonight.'

An instant frown invaded her face. 'What you mean? You have to go to the game. Don't be stupid. Luigi will be angry ...'

'There is somebody ...' He cleared his throat. 'I have to see somebody.'

'Somebody? You have nobody!' she said, throwing her hands up. But then her gaze came to rest on the *Leader* newspaper sprawled across the kitchen bench. A photo of a young man stared back at her. She moved closer to the paper. 'Joseph Lorenzo exhibition at Brunswick gallery,' she read out. 'Joseph Lorenzo? You telling me you go to this gallery tonight?' She shook her head. 'You are a stupid man.'

'Why I stupid, you stupid woman? All you want me to do is waste my money and— '

'Waste you money?' she said, stepping closer to him. 'I no force you to do it. You see me hold gun to you head? No! And you are stupid if you think he will want to see you after all these years.'

'He is older now,' he said, lowering his voice. 'He will understand.'

'There is nothing to understand. He will laugh at you. The world laughs at you, Francesco. And if you no come to the game tonight, I no be surprised if I find you dead.'

'Then you go to the game for me. Tell Luigi I see him tomorrow. Tell him I go and see my son.'

His 1979 Ford Laser chugged and chugged as he backed out of his car spot, then stalled. Esmeralda had followed him outside. She stood and watched, shaking her head. Francesco stared at his hands clutched over the steering wheel. No car, no way of going to the gallery. He sighed. It was time to stop, time to surrender and resume his meaningless existence. He glanced at the *Leader* newspaper on the passenger seat. Joseph's photo smiled back at him.

'Daddy, Daddy, the birds are coming, Daddy.' Joseph was tugging at Francesco's trousers.

The waves of The Great Ocean Road roared in magnificence. It was the first warm day of spring and Lorne beach was bustling with families escaping the city, happy that the harsh winter had drifted into oblivion for yet another year. Everyone around them seemed to be in bloom, the warm sun shining on pale faces. Francesco and his wife held hands.

'Run, Joseph, run, try to catch them ...' Francesco motioned him forward and Joseph sprinted towards the pigeons.

'You can't catch birds, Daddy,' Maria said, her hands firm on her hips, pigtails springing from the sides of her head.

Francesco released his wife's hand and squatted by Maria. 'I tell you a special secret?'

Maria's eyes widened. 'Tell me, Daddy.'

'Sometimes, if you wish for something and believe, it will come true.'

'Really, Daddy?'

Francesco smiled. 'Yes. It can take a long time, but you have to believe. If you no try then you never know if you can.'

Maria nodded, licking her lips. 'Okay, Daddy. I'll get a bird, okay? I'll bring it to you, okay?'

'Okay, Bella. You go and get the bird.'

And so, barefoot, along the sandy shore of the ocean, she ran after the seagulls, trying to catch her bird, giggling as the salty water tickled her feet, oblivious to the complication of life ...

Rain drizzled onto the windshield. Francesco grabbed the *Leader* in his hand and opened the door. He did not look at Esmeralda. Instead he exited the car and started walking out of the carpark and onto the footpath. Esmeralda called after him but Francesco, he just kept walking. The rain morphed from drizzle into splatter, more and more of it came, a vehement, angry rain working against him, a rain demanding that he not go, that he had no right, but still Francesco continued.

The train, he thought to himself, I catch the train.

He hadn't caught the train for twenty years and now he knew why. Not only was the ticketing system too complicated for him to understand, but the lady behind the window seemed annoyed that he did not know how to use it. She chewed on gum while stressing the importance of him having to do something with his ticket, *validibate? vali-cate?* And in the end, because he did not understand, she huffed and came out from behind her window, inserting the ticket he purchased into a zapping machine that sucked it in then spat it out.

'Why you need to do this?'

Her gaze lowered, and that's when Francesco noticed the water dripping from his suit. She gave him a puzzled expression, wiggled her nose like she had just picked up a whiff of him. 'Because that's how things work.'

A puddle was forming. 'Where is your bathroom?'

She raised one eyebrow, her jaw springing on the gum. 'Behind you, mate.'

The men's bathroom smelled strongly of urine. But there was a hand-dryer on the wall. Francesco unzipped his pants and removed them. He squeezed the water out of them then placed them under the warm air of the dryer.

As he dried, the door flew open, startling Francesco. A young man with porcupine hair and an overblown sports jacket halted at the sight of Francesco in his white underwear.

'I dry—'

'Hey, dude,' the youth said, raising his hands in defence, 'whatever works for you, dude.' He entered a cubicle, slammed the door behind him.

Francesco quickly put his pants back on then dried his jacket until an announcement came over the speakers: *The next train to depart on platform one will be the 5:57 Flinders Street, stopping all stations, to Flinders Street*. Francesco put on his jacket. It was still wet, weighing heavily on his shoulders.

The dim street lights did little to calm him as he walked the night. At least it had stopped raining. His underarms were damp, and he could smell his off-putting body odour. It nauseated him. The sweat dripped from his forehead. He repeatedly wiped it with the sleeve of his jacket. He was late. So late. Too late. He had to go to Flinders Street Station then take another train. Not only that but he did not know exactly where he was going. Once again he had been idiotic and not used his head. He *should* have asked for directions at Jewel Station. Instead he decided he was capable of finding his own way.

The heels of Francesco's shoes tapped against the old cobblestones of Brunswick. He turned a corner and there it was, as he knew it would be—a dead end. How he ended up in a laneway he did not know. He pressed on his chest to numb the pain. The day was too much for his heart, more than the stresses of gambling. He needed an extra tablet of his heart medication but he hadn't brought any with him, another stupid oversight. Francesco took a few deep breaths, somewhat calming himself. He would have to retrace his steps back to Jewel Station.

After some helpful directions from a young Italian man at the station, Francesco made it to Sydney Road. There were beeping cars, a tram ringing its bell, and pedestrians running across the street. The historic Brunswick Town Hall stood tall in the distance with its clock, declaring the time for all of Brunswick to see. Francesco clutched the *Leader* newspaper, but it was soft from the rain, was slowly disintegrating. He gently opened it to check the address. The Counihan Gallery was next to the town hall. He continued along Sydney Road.

The entrance of the gallery was made of glass. Above the revolving doors, two thin, yellow legs stepped out into nothingness. People in conservative attire walked past him and into the gallery, their sweetness and cleanliness lingering in the night air. A man with curly hair was handing out fliers for the exhibition. Francesco stopped. The world around him was melting into a blur. He clutched his forehead.

'Are you alright, Mister?' the man asked.

Francesco blinked a few times and the man came into focus again. He nodded.

'Are you here for the exhibition?'

Just then another young man came outside and patted the curly-haired man on the shoulder. 'You luring people in, Chris?'

'Shut up, man,' Chris said, nudging the other man.

Francesco studied the young man who had come from inside. He was fumbling for something in his jacket. He retrieved a packet of cigarettes from his pocket. This man was Joseph. Francesco smiled, tears forming in the corners of his eyes. Joseph, oblivious to Francesco's emotional response, chatted with his friend. Francesco was silent, drinking in the vision of Joseph; the perfection of his features, the way his wavy hair parted to the side, the maturity in his large, confronting eyes. If Francesco had wanted anything for Joseph when he was a young boy, it was to become the man who stood before him. In that moment Francesco wanted to stand tall, to take care of himself, to not gamble, to be clean and proud. He had done the right thing. Joseph was everything he had wanted him to be.

Joseph flicked his lighter, inhaled from his cigarette. 'I *so* needed one of these,' he said to Chris. Joseph's gaze lingered on his father, the smirk on his face, dwindling. 'Um … sorry … you look *really* familiar. Have we met?'

Francesco opened his mouth but before he could speak, Joseph's eyes narrowed. A vicious anger began to spread over his face. 'You're not … ?'

Francesco extended his hand but Joseph took a quick step back. 'Dad?' he forced out in disgust. '*My* dad?' he said. 'You're fucking kidding me.'

'Joseph.'

Joseph shook his head hard, his face bitter, like he had just sculled a glass of vinegar. 'Don't give me that shit. I don't want to see you.'

Francesco smiled with semi-optimism, motioned towards the revolving door. 'Please, I am you father. Take me into the gallery, show me you art.'

Joseph tossed his unfinished cigarette to the ground. 'Show you my art, old man? Show you my *art*?' Joseph chuckled, but it was an insane sort of chuckle that turned into a hysterical sort of a laugh, and then Chris was laughing, and so Francesco joined in, because he wasn't sure if he should laugh or cry.

'Come, Joseph, let's go and look. I am so proud—'

'Don't you get it, old man?' he said, his words like blades. 'You don't exist to me.' Joseph stepped closer, dug a finger into Francesco's chest. 'You've got the fucking nerve to show your face here after walking out on us? You're fucking joking right?' He looked at his friend. 'This is a dream right? A dream? A fucking nightmare, yeah?'

Chris patted Joseph's shoulder. 'Calm down, Joseph.'

'I write you letters,' Francesco said.

'There were no fucking letters. There was nothing for fifteen years.'

Francesco shook his hands out in front of him in a panicked, disorientated manner. 'You mother … she must keep them from you …'

'Don't you dare bring Mum into this after what you did to her, cheating on her with all those women. You hit her. You even … You *did* things to her—this is so fucked. We may have been too young to understand back then but she filled us in on all of it, told us everything we needed to know.'

'Ask her about the letters if you no believe me,' he said, taking a hold of Joseph's forearm, but Joseph shrugged it off.

'You're a coward. That's what you are.'

'I just want to—'

'Wanted to what? Ruin my night? You know what? Get the fuck out of my sight. Go on,' he said, motioning him back until Francesco was stumbling on his feet, 'fuck off.'

The tears were now streaming freely down Francesco's face, and his heart, oh, his heart, it hurt so much, so very much, and although his facial expression pleaded with Joseph, Joseph's face was hard, unforgiving. There was so much Francesco wanted to say, but the more time he spent looking at Joseph's face, the queasier he became. And so Francesco gave a few weak nods, turned around, and began the long journey back to Reservoir, his hand pressing on his chest all the way home.

The door to his flat was unlocked but he didn't hesitate to go inside. The phone was ringing too, as he stumbled into the darkness. He knew it was either Esmeralda, to nag about the game, or Luigi to threaten him about the money.

'Esmeralda!'

There was no answer. Esmeralda must have forgotten to lock the door, he thought. Francesco sobbed beyond comprehension, his hand still pressing on the excruciating pain in his chest, his teeth chattering as the harsh cold in the flat blanketed him. It was colder inside than out. Much colder.

Francesco went to the bathroom to retrieve his heart medication. But it wasn't in its usual place. He never moved it from its usual place. He stumbled to the living room, checked the coffee table, under some papers on the couch. Nothing. Maybe his bedroom. His bedroom. The phone continued to ring. It would not stop. It was not on his bedside table! He made his way up onto his bed and closed his eyes. He tried to force his mind to warm places, The Great Ocean Road. He wanted to see their smiling faces. Oh, what he would give to live that moment again. He would take Joseph and Maria in his arms and kiss them over and over again, showering them with words of love and affection, and he would never let them go. But no matter how much Francesco tried, their smiling faces would not come to him. Instead he saw Joseph and Maria with hard, unforgiving faces. He tried to erase their angry faces but they would not leave him, their bitterness pulsing through his blood stream like poison, circulating through his body, crushing his heart.

'I will not stop.' His ex-wife screamed in Italian. It was retribution that she craved.

He pounded the kitchen table with his fist. 'Shut up, you crazy woman! You're scaring the children.'

Joseph and Maria ran into the bedroom sobbing, slamming the door behind them.

'See what you do,' he said, pointing towards bedroom. 'Every time I come to see them you do this. You like to make them cry like this?'

'You are the one making them cry by coming here. When you are not here, they are happy. When they are not thinking when you will visit next, they are happy.'

'I visit when I visit.'

'You visit when you are not playing cards.'

'Why you care what I do in my time? I don't love you. You don't love me. But we love Joseph and Maria.'

She shook her head. 'You do not love them. If you did you would not hurt them all the time like this. You would not disappoint them.'

'I have to see my children!'

'For who, Francesco? For them or for you?'

The scene looped in his mind, jumbled images and distorted audio, and then something was cutting into his breath, like a guillotine, cutting it shorter and shorter and shorter, suffocating his cries, and shorter, and shorter, until there was a hiss, just a hiss, a hiss, then a silence, and a stop. Stop. The stop. The nothing. He died. Francesco was dead. But his cry kept on, leaving his body to become an entity, a ghost of its very own. And to this day, when the cold is so bitter it freezes bones; on nights when the craving for familiarity is essential to keep breathing, on those nights his cries can be heard, echoing through the run-down flats in that quiet street nobody wants to walk down in Reservoir.

11.

Bad Italian Girl

When I was young I wanted to move out of home, but Dad said he'd kill me if I did so I stayed put. *Cattiva ragazza Italiana*—Bad Italian girl—is what he'd call me when I did something he didn't approve of. Maybe I *was* bad. I did have sex with Nick in the backseat of his Commodore, but Dad never found out about that. Lucky—he would have killed me. When he said it, I think he was more referring to incidents like when I wore *putana* skirts, or skipped school, or when he caught me having a ciggie by the side fence. He bashed the shit out of me for that. Mum said it was all my fault. Maybe it was.

Mum never said it but I think she also thought it was my fault my *zio* put his thing in me. This *zio* wasn't blood related, just a friend of the family from my dad's village in Sicily that we grew up with. When I was old enough to put two-and-two together and realise it *was* actually wrong what he was doing to me, there was lots of whispering in the night between my parents and then we never saw my *zio* and his family again. They moved back to Italy. I remember really missing my cousin but neither of us reached out. Dad was never able to look me in the eyes after that. Occasionally though, his gaze accidentally crossed with mine, and I saw it—the flicker of shame.

Apart from the conversation with Mum, nobody spoke about it. I don't think my sister or my brothers found out. My parents didn't want anyone to find out—not my cousins, not my friends, not anyone in the Italian community. People talk. Judge. What would they think of me?

Or worse, my parents? No scandal, no shame. They just wanted the whole thing forgotten. And it was, for the most part.

Those were the days in Coburg where all the ethnic chicks snuck around behind their parents' back doing stuff they knew they shouldn't be doing. It was a race to the altar, a sprint to outdo each other—the ritziest wedding, the biggest dress, the hottest guy of your own kind.

Nick and I met at a wedding when I was nineteen. His dad and my mum were from the same village so I had the ultimate catch. There was lots of envy for what I had among the Italian girls I knew but I—for the most part—pretended not to notice. I was a bit of a catch myself. I'm not skinny, but I've got massive green eyes and really thick, long brown hair. I was pursuing acting at the time, had a few speaking roles in films that went to the cinema, and was also in a few plays. I was just always really good at it, and I loved playing someone else. I liked to write stories too. I had this blue journal and I wrote so much stuff in it.

When Nick and I started going out we had to keep it a secret because I wasn't allowed to have a boyfriend and my parents would kill me if they found out. I'd just go out with a bunch of my friends and he'd go out with a bunch of his mates and we'd escape to the dark heart of Melbourne, Metro nightclub on Friday nights. After about six months we told our parents. They were all pushing pretty hard that we get married. Mum and Dad were saying I can't roam the streets with a man because it wasn't right. At twenty-one—he was twenty-three—we got married.

Nick's parents straight away said I had to give up the acting to focus on my husband and creating a family. I didn't really care. I was just relieved to finally be moving out of home. I felt so free. Nick and I we moved into his parents' place so we could save money for a house. Nick had started up his own mechanic shop and business was picking up. My sister-in-law had a hairdressing salon in the shed out the back and I went and did a course in hairdressing and started working with her.

Nick and I eventually got our own place in Preston, a few streets away from my in-laws. It worked out well because I was close to the salon, and the plan was that when we eventually had kids, the in-laws could look after them, and of course my parents would help too.

I always knew Nick had a temper. He never hurt me, but when he yelled at me, I hated that. I would just shut up because I wasn't really good at people yelling at me. If I shut up he was okay. Mostly he got angry if someone did something to upset me. I liked that he was all protective over me, it made me feel safe, special. I thought, you know, women need a man to look after them. But after we got the new house and we had more bills, he was getting angry more. Then when I accidentally forgot to take the pill and got pregnant he went psycho:

'You did it on purpose,' he yelled in my face and he was pulling at my hair, like really fucking pulling it.

'Nick … why would I do that, man?'

'Because you're stupid, Lisa, that's why.'

'Let go, Nick, let go.'

He did let go, and I was crying and he just left the house. He snuck in as the sun was coming up, drunk, crawled under the bedsheets and was crying and kissing me. 'Sorry, babe, sorry.'

Of course I forgave him. He was my husband and I loved him.

When I gave birth to Nicole things were hard. I was crying a lot. I couldn't understand why. I told myself, you should be happy. This is what you always wanted. All the other Italian girls are jealous of you. But I still kept crying and crying. My parents and my in-laws helped heaps and I started seeing my parents different, like I kind of understood where they were coming from a bit. I stopped working at the salon and stayed home to do all the house stuff and look after Nicole.

Every now and then though, I thought about my acting days and how much I loved it. I missed it so much, living in someone else's skin, in their story. The older Nicole got, the more I craved it. I looked into what courses were around. When Nicole was around two, I bought it up with Nick one night at dinner.

'Why?' he asked.

'Just to get out of the house a bit. You know, clear my head. Mum said she'd look after Nicole.' But I hadn't even asked Mum yet. I just knew it would be easier if I got his okay first, because Mum would say yes if Nick said yes.

'So it's just one night a week?'

'Yeah. A short course in theatre.'

'Okay. If you feel like it'll help you be happier, why not?'

Mum didn't want me to do the course because she knew my in-laws wouldn't like it. But when I told her Nick said *yes,* she said she'd babysit but I could tell she didn't like it. 'Focus on your family and stop climbing to the sky because one day you are going to fall and break your face,' she said to me in Italian. I tried not to buy into her trap and nodded. She could say whatever. As long I was doing the course, I was happy.

What was so awesome about the course was not only the weird people I met, like Australians who were free and wild, but also that they taught us how to write theatre and TV scripts as well as act. It was so cool because apart from *Acropolis Now* in the 90s, there were no other shows about us wogs on TV and I had heaps of ideas.

I made so many new friends and got invited to parties and gatherings. I wanted Nick to come along too but he just wanted to stay home and watch the soccer, or hang out with his mates and play cards. On nights we were both out, Mum and Dad would baby-sit, but they'd always be lecturing me on what people would think if I'm out without my husband.

'I don't care what people think.'

'We do, you see!' Mum would say. And Dad was so pissed he wouldn't even talk to me.

But I just kept doing the course. I even started auditioning for roles. When I got a call one day from a producer offering me a role in a pretty big production that was going to tour around Australia I was so excited I had to stop myself from calling Nick at work and blabbing. I bit my tongue and kept myself busy until that night. I made his favourite for dinner, spaghetti bolognaise, and I waited until Nicole was in bed and we were on the couch.

'It's called *Breaking Out* and I'm gonna play Simara, babe.'

He had his feet outstretched, was flicking through channels. 'What d'you mean? You can't do that.'

'Huh?'

'How you gonna tour? You got Nicole.'

'My parents, your parents—we can make it work.'

'Nah, I don't want you to do it.'

I had to stop a minute, because I couldn't understand why he was even saying that. 'But why? I want to have a career too. Why can't I?'

'Career? You got a career as a hairdresser. You never said nothing about a career when you said about doing this course. You said it was a hobby.'

'I never said that.'

'I don't care what you said. That's what I thought you meant. If you do this, then you'll get something else, and something else, and it's gonna get outta hand.'

'But I want to, babe.'

But he just got up and pretended like I didn't say nothing. 'I'm going to bed. Night.'

It took me a few days to kind of process what he said. I knew my parents would agree with him. I didn't tell my new friends at school what was going on because I didn't feel like we had that kind of relationship. I told my younger sister, Francesca.

'It's so awesome you got that, but Nick's right. You got responsibilities. All that acting stuff has to come *after* your kids and your house. You made a choice to have a kid, and now you got to raise that kid. Plus I thought you wanted to have another one.'

'I do.'

'So ...'

'But I feel like I got all this stuff I want to say.'

'We all got stuff we want to say. But Lisa, who's gonna care what you say?'

I didn't really want to get out of bed after that convo with Francesca. I wasn't talking much either. I stopped going to the course. Some of my friends tried to ring me but I didn't respond. I stopped eating. I started losing all this weight. Nick took me to the doctors and the doctor put me on some pills. I didn't know if I should take them but it was as if I was up against a wall with nowhere to go.

Slowly time went on and I started eating and getting better but I felt pretty flat inside. Not happy, not sad, just flat. I got back into working at the salon. There was nothing much that excited me so I said okay when Nick said to try for another baby. Nicole was four. But I had to come off the meds to start trying for a baby.

The first week was hell. I couldn't stop crying. I felt like my insides were trying to claw out of me. It did cross my mind to kill myself. But I thought I couldn't, because of Nicole. The pill doctor told me to write my thoughts down to help with withdrawal.

It didn't take me long to really get into the writing. I couldn't stop. And I didn't, even after my son Gino was born. I wrote every chance I could. I was writing and writing and I wrote a play and a few episodes for a TV show idea I got. I imagined myself playing the lead. It was called *Bad Italian Girl*.

Is it the writer writing the story or the story writing the writer? I think it was the latter for me. The more I wrote, and dreamed, and wanted more, the angrier Nick became. I researched feminism and how much women struggled and fought and died just so women could have equal rights to vote. Every word I wrote opened my mind up more and more. It was as if my entire life I was only operating in a small section of my mind, and now that section was widening. There was so much to catch up on, so much to learn, so much more to fight for.

My fights with Nick became repetitive. He hit me. He abused me. He raped me. My uncle raped me. My dad repeatedly hit me. I have had these statements closeted in my chest for years, never able to vocalise them, but now I can. I stood in front of a mirror on day, when Nick wasn't home, and the children were at my mum's, and I said them, I said, *I am a victim of domestic violence.*

Then one night there was a fight, I can't even remember how it started, but Nick took our wedding photo and smashed it, and in that moment, when the glass shattered, I knew in that moment, I was leaving him. I was crying and he was yelling something like 'do you understand? Do you?' and he was pulling at my hair and I was nodding and saying 'yes, yes' and he was like 'I can't hear you' and I was saying 'yes, yes, yes' but in my mind I was thinking I'm going to do it. I'm going to go. I'm going to get out of this fucking life. I didn't choose this *life*.

Fuck the ethnics, fuck the wogs. Fuck them all to hell. I'm leaving.

I didn't trust him not to do something to me if I left, so I had to have everything ready. I actually got back in touch with a friend from the course, Kelly, and told her my story. I asked if she could help me because she was also a single mum. Nobody else in my life I knew would help me or understand. They would all make me stay or they'd go and tell Nick what I was up to. Kelly said she had a spare room in her house and I could stay there with the kids until I sorted myself out. I opened a bank account in my name. Then I had to do it all in one day while he was at work. I packed up as much stuff as I could in two suitcases, for me and the kids. I transferred $5,000 into my account because that's as much as I could transfer without him signing too. I went and picked up Nicole from school with Gino, and we left. I didn't tell anyone. I changed my mobile phone number. Nobody knew where I was. I left a note on the kitchen table. *I want a divorce. I will be in touch. Lisa.*

When I got the strength to ring my sister Francesca a week later, she was yelling at me on the phone that I am completely fucked.

'You're just a spoilt shit who's had everything handed to her on a silver platter and now she's sick of that platter and she's asking for different platters. You think you're gonna be some famous actress? You're dreaming.'

'I just want to live my life,' I said really level, but my hands were shaking, and the kids were upset, crying and watching me. I'd never told my family Nick abused me. I didn't want to. Why did it matter? Was I only allowed to leave if I was being abused? Women should just be able to leave if they feel like it's the best for them, no explanations. This is what feminism is. But even though my sister was younger and threw the word feminism around, I don't think she got what it really meant.

'You're so selfish. And you know who's gonna pay? The kids. And don't be surprised if you give Dad a heart attack. He's not coping.

If something happens to him it'll be all your fault. So go and be an actress, everything's always been about you.'

The guilt flooded me, occupied every cell in my body. My parents said they would never love me again if I didn't go back. Nick said he wasn't going to give me a cent, and he wouldn't sign the form confirming our separation so I could get a single mother's pension. Money was so tight for a while. I got a restraining order on him. It was a long, messy and painful divorce and it took almost two years for everything to be cleared up and for me and the kids to feel safe. I ended up in hospital three times from the stress. I married him when I was 21 and left when I was 35.

Four years later and I can say my old life and pain is behind me. My life is my own. Thirty-nine years old with a twelve-year-old and an eight-year-old on my shoulders, trying to play catch up. Starting my life at thirty-nine. I feel like a child sometimes too.

I have my own salon. The divorce settlement helped with that. It's in Northcote, on High Street, where all the shops are. I've got a full-timer, Elise, and an apprentice, Nina. I didn't really want to go back into hairdressing. I just wanted to work on my acting and my writing. To tell our stories, the female stories. To make a difference. To help women. But I needed to make money, I had to work. I haven't given up though. I work at the salon all day and write most nights. I average about five hours of sleep.

At the salon, I'm putting some foils in for Dimitra, one of my regulars, when my iPhone vibrates. It's flashing "Derek".

'Lisa, you can answer it, babe,' Dimitra says.

'I'll call him back on my break, darl, don't worry about it.' I separate out another strand of hair, lay it over a piece of foil and brush it with some hair colouring.

'Him? Tell me more please.'

'As if, Dimitra. I got no time for a man. I haven't even got time to sleep let alone find time for a man.'

'Yeah, but we all need a bit of loving, Lisa.'

I laugh. 'Darl, I'm too old for love. My kids give me all the love I need.'

'There's love, Lisa. You just gotta be open to it.'

Dimitra's one of my more open customers. I hate it when I got to fake smile to those customers that I know judge me because I'm a single mum. They don't say it, but I can just tell in the way they speak to me, like their life is "the normal life" and they can't really make sense of whatever it is I seem to be doing. For those clients I ask them more about their own life and don't say much about mine. It's the same with my family, cousins, aunts, uncles—anyone in the Italian community. It's better to keep your real self buried so nobody feels too uncomfortable.

After finishing Dimitra's foils, I go out back. I was lucky with this place. There's a small square of outdoor space with a shed, toilet and laundry. There's even a plum tree. I sit on the steps, light up a ciggie and call Derek.

'Lisa! How's my favourite Italian girl?'

'Good, Derek. Just on my break at the salon. What's up?'

'They want to option the TV show!'

'What? Are you serious? My TV show?'

'Yep. They want to draw up contracts for *Bad Italian Girl*.'

'*What?*'

'Come into my office next week and we'll sit down with the contract. Good work.'

After the phone convo, I'm holding my phone and my hands are shaking. I finish my ciggie then I light up another one. I get tears in my eyes. I try to stop them but they come. I can't get up. I can't move.

I thought when we got rejected from the ethnic channel broadcaster that was it for *Bad Italian Girl*. It was two Anglo women who rejected me. An ethnic channel run by Anglos. What a joke. I thought it was over. I thought I'd missed the boat.

'Lisa? Do you want me to rinse out Dimitra's foils?' Elise calls from the front.

I get up quick. 'Sorry, I'm coming.'

It's morning and the alarm's gone off. I've snoozed at least five times. My feet hurt, my back aches. We live upstairs from the salon. Nicole and Gino share a room. I can hear them conversing from their beds.

I couldn't sleep last night. I couldn't stop thinking about my meeting with Derek. I thought I'd missed the boat, but Kelly, she was the one who told me I should send some footage of my previous acting to an agent. Derek took me on straight away, said there was something about me he couldn't put his finger on, just something. I'm just living off the salon money and a bit of savings. I've applied for grants and funding for my writing with no luck. But if *Bad Italian Girl* actually gets made I could make money and keep writing. I could tell more stories and help more women.

Since I signed with Derek six months ago I got one commercial, which was good money. There aren't many acting jobs for us wog ethnics though. In the meantime he'd been showing my TV show idea to some production companies. I didn't expect nothing from it, me acting and writing my own TV show. I watch TV shows and everything is white Anglo. Everything. The actors, the stories, everything. And all the ethnics who happen to get on TV—that are writing their own stuff—are guys. The books too—guys. The only stand-out ethnic chick I could think of was Effie from *Acropolis Now,* but she was playing dumb. Where are all the smart women? Are they all trapped like I was? Makes me wish I was a guy. Did *they* ever have to make ham and cheese sandwiches for their sisters or their mum? Did they have all that push to be good and get married and have kids? Yeah they had to get married too but they had more choices than us girls. Every time I see an ethnic guy on TV I want to punch him in the face. What did we get, us girls? We got encouraged to stay dumb, to learn to cook and clean, and be good housewives. At least the guys got to fuck around and live. Now I can't even do that. Too fucked up, too damaged for any of that. Missed the boat with love, but maybe, maybe it's not too late for my career.

'Mum—get up! GET UP!' It's Gino, and he's shaking me.

I want to sleep forever. 'I will, just one more minute ...'

'We're going to be late for school, Mum.'

'Mum, move your butt!' Nicole shouts.

Gino's pulling my arm.

'Okay, okay.'

I get them ready, put on a nice dress, take them to school then head off to fancy Prahran to meet with Derek. Prahran, the "big business" suburb, where all the rich actors live.

In Derek's office, the receptionist tells me to take a seat. Every time I come here I always look at the photos of all the famous actors on the walls. Lots of young girls. Girls that started acting at fifteen and have been working at their craft every day for ten years. I will have to make up for lost time. I will work at double the speed, three times as fast. I have to catch up.

'Lisa, how's my favourite girl?' Derek says when he comes out of his office.

He always brings a giddy smile to my face. Sometimes I have to pinch myself that he's my agent, that famous people that I watch on TV are represented by him.

'Hi, Derek!'

'Come in, come in,' he enthuses.

We sit at his round table. There's a contract on it.

'Can I get you a glass of water?'

'Yes, please.'

I drink as soon as he hands it to me.

'So, how've you been?'

'Salon and salon and kids. Writing some more.'

'Good to hear. Now, I've had a look at the contract, and we just need to go over a few things.'

'Okay…'

'Big Productions really love the writing, and they want you to write it, they're going to get you to work with an experienced writing team, and you'll co-write with a very well-known writer, John Barnes—'

'John Barnes?'

'I know, but he's really good, and he'll help you develop your writing skills.'

I take a moment. 'Co-write? It's my story.'

'Think of him as a mentor. I've only heard good things about him.'

Maybe it's not so bad. I hope there will be at least some wogs on the writing team. 'I guess it's okay …'

'Good. Now … they also have some reservations about the acting.'

I sit back, take another sip of water. 'They don't want me, right?'

'It's not your ability, they just want to go with someone a bit … younger.'

I don't know what to say. Is this what success is? 'Can I smoke?'

'Sorry?'

'In here, can I smoke?'

'Not really, but … you can, it's okay.' He gets up, retrieves an ashtray from his bottom draw, like he's been in situations like this before.

I retrieve a ciggie from my purse, a layer of tears welling, but I keep them in, I keep composed. There's a slight tremor in my hands. I light up, take a deep drag. I've been waiting so many years for this moment. I should be happy, not disappointed. There are women who would dream to be in my position. I should be thankful. Okay, so I won't ever have my poster up on the wall in Derek's entryway. Okay so my upbringing fucked up my life. But at least I made it here. At least I survived. I survived and I made it, I made it here.

'I don't want you to take this the wrong way … I think you're a great actor, and I'm confident you'll get a role that's right for you … '

I take another drag …

'This is a great opportunity for you. It'll be great for your career.'

'Do you agree with them?'

He pauses, looks me straight in the eyes. He slowly nods. 'I've talked to them. They're not going to budge. You don't have to do anything you don't want to do. But I think you should take it. Opportunities like these don't come by often for …'

'For people like me.'

Silence.

'You can take some time to think about it.'

I butt my ciggie in the ashtray. 'No, it's okay. Where do I sign?'

12.

Player

You know you are a player, this you know. But you're okay with it. You know you're not the most attractive man, a 'stud', as someone might say. You're an average height, reasonable build, a little beer gut, but you're working on that. At your age, the body starts to slow down, but you're on top of that now with the gym membership. The early mornings are a killer, but it'll all be worth it in the long run. You've got good arms, large and firm, and the chicks love that, love to give them a little squeeze. But it's your eyes that are the winner: icy-blue. The chicks take one look into them and they're hooked, like gazing across Antarctic glaciers. You don't mind that you're plain looking—it actually works in your favour. From past experience you know that great looking, insecure women tend to give average blokes like you a second glance: someone to sleep with, have some fun without getting too attached, because she can do so much better. So she'll just have a play while she waits for Mr Right. But they are the ones, oh yes, they are the ones that always get attached, because they have no idea how smart you really are. You're really, really smart.

After travelling with your music for ten years, exploring everything there is to explore in the realms of sex, and fucking so many women you've lost count (and the occasional man), you decided it was time to come home to Sydney. A mate's offer of an account management position in his new logistics company sealed the deal. You'd never had a nine-to-five job, and you knew nothing about business, but after ten years of jumping from cruise ship to cruise ship you wanted a house, a place to call your own. You were up for a new challenge and you were sick of being broke. A year later, you're loving it, and so it seems do the women: 'I'm focusing on my career right now, I don't have time for a relationship...' And you don't! It's a steep learning curve. It's all about expectations, you tell yourself, and you say the same to all the women—and there *are* women. You've collated a bank of them, a list in your iPhone, you're really proud of that list. You're always upfront: we hang out, we sleep together, but this isn't a relationship. I'm seeing other people and you can see other people. It's totally casual.

Smooth and casual.

The dating websites were the best invention for players like you. You've done the routine so many times you've lost count, and it works. It works almost every time. You chat with many women—you never have your eye on only one, that's danger territory. You like to get to know them first, find out what their interests are, but you always wait for *them* to ask *you* out, because that's how you know you've fished an insecure one.

On the first coffee date you know within minutes what she's thinking—you're very good at reading people. You already know she thinks she can do better. But you're attentive, ask questions about her life—geeze, you're a nice bloke! You enjoy getting to know them. You try not to get too affectionate though, but you can't help it, there's a part of you that wants to connect, and even though you can see in their eyes that they think you're a nice, insightful guy, you also see that glint of wanting time to accelerate so the date can be over. But, you can't help it, you love people, and your old friends had mostly moved on by the time you moved back home, so you talk and talk till it gets a bit too much and you abruptly end the date. You're a working man, you need your sleep. But you always give them a tight hug because you're just like a teddy bear. You really enjoy a cuddle.

When you get home, if she's made an impression, you get your cock out and stroke it, imagine fucking her in all sorts of positions. Then the chase begins. You send a thoughtful sms in a few days, one that shows you were listening to what she was saying, ask if she's free again, if not, you'll catch up with her soon.

For example, Emmy. She's recently divorced. Married young to escape her controlling Greek family. It was pretty clear from the get go that she was dealing with a shit-load. On your first date a few days ago she mentioned a family function on the weekend. So you smsed her to say if she needs an escape afterwards you're more than happy to meet.

She took the bait, of course. You meet her in the city for drinks and she looks even hotter the second time around. You're chatting away and before you know it she's missed the last tram and she's stressed out (poor thing!). You caught the train in so you offer to drive her home if she rides with you to yours (no funny business). You always do the right thing by them, always the gentleman, wait for them to make the move. She agrees, and so you're chatting away again on the empty train, except there's this weirdo that looks at you funny, and you can see Emmy's spooked out too, so you put your arm around her and the weirdo backs off and Emmy seems glad.

When you get to your place you're ready to hop in your car to drive her when she says 'I'd love to hear you play some piano' (yeah, right) so you say 'sure', and you both go inside. You make her tea in your nan's antique kettle. Emmy's eyes are so sweet and kind, and ... empathic, and as she's talking to you, telling you her amazing life story, everything she's overcome, you decide right there that you really want to get to know her, not just sleep with her. She's been through a rough time lately, what she needs is a friend. So you play the piano for her, and while you're both sitting on the couch, you rest your head on her shoulder, and then a thought suddenly shudders through you, the thought that she's special.

'It's getting late, maybe I should take you home?'

'But don't you want to kiss me?' she grins.

Her words hurt you for a second, but then you're smiling, and then you're kissing her, and her lips are so soft, but you're hesitating, because you're not sure about this one, you're not sure about Emmy. At the end of the day they just want to get into your pants, because they think they can do it and be unattached, but they always get attached, always. They can't help it, they're women, and if she wants to play, if she just wants to fuck you without knowing you, then you can play that game, you can play that game really, really well.

You know you are a player, this, you know. And you're comfortable with that term, it keeps you sane, safe. When they bypass your personality and reach for your cock then you're in predictable, controlling territory. You've been with so many women you're sure you're in the thousands. You've studied women like a scientist in a laboratory. It's easy. You may not be the best looking man, but fucking, you've mastered. You only fuck them if you have two hours. If you fuck them quickly and they don't have at least one intense orgasm, then it's not worth your effort. The stronger the orgasm, the deeper their brain path is wired to you, the deeper the attachment. So you fuck them properly, only once a session, and not too often—you always leave them wanting more.

You know how to make them come just by sucking on their nipples, although Emmy, she's a weird one, she never lets you suck her nipples and you have to fight her, even after you tell her repeatedly that you love to suck them. In fact, this angry Greek girl who's only slept with two other guys is always fighting you in bed. You don't mind it though, you have some of your own battles to fight.

You give the best head and you know it. You've mastered it like an art-form and the girls come and come, although not Emmy. You try hard but you can't get her to come that way, but you can in other ways, and all you need is for her to have one mind-blowing orgasm, so she keeps coming back for more. She is a weird one that Emmy, screamed the whole house down last week. In fact, in your vast experience, you've never quite encountered someone like her. And you've been with a lot of women!

After sleeping with a chick a few times, the girl, so addicted to the fucking, may want to possess you. If this happens you're quick to drop the whole thing. Your job is number one—you've got no time for drama. So you send a long email, you put effort into it, because you enjoy writing, and you want them to understand it's just that you are both too different and all you can offer is a casual sex situation. You explain that you'd like to remain friends but you think it's best they stay out of contact for a while. It's not your fault if the girl then accepts the offer because she'll take what she can get. It's all about expectations. You're not a dishonest person!

From there, it's smooth sailing. You get at least five messages from different girls a week. You respond to each one only *once*, and you say, very businesslike, that perhaps they could meet on such and such night, maybe. But you don't confirm till the last minute because you're not sure which girl you'll feel like seeing. You meet with them at weird hours, like after a gig at 1am, because you still play your music on weekends, you need it to survive. You fuck them properly but you never spend the night. You're romantic, always—this isn't just fucking. You're a gentle, considerate lover (except with Emmy, but that's because she fights). If at any point during the courtship the woman discloses she has her period, you note the date in your iPhone later.

It's important information. When you know woman x is having her period she won't mind if you say you're busy, because all she wants is a fuck, and she can't because she's got her period, so she's not going to kick up a stink, and then you can just go fuck someone else.

You disappear all the time, and that's just you, and the women don't know where and they don't need to—it's none of their business. If you wanted a girlfriend, you'd get one, it's not that hard. You don't owe them anything. You'll answer their messages when you have time and when you feel like it. The most important thing in your life is your career, building your foundation, stability. The women come to accept that it's part of the deal for you giving them the best fuck of their lives. This is how you operate, this is who you are, and if they don't like it they can stop seeing you, that's okay with you because you've got an entire bank of women. When they freak out and send abusive messages you ignore them. You don't need to put up with that hurtful shit. If that happens you don't contact them again unless they apologise, and you always forgive, because you're a forgiving bloke.

You can't help it, but sometimes, you get attached. It's not in the plan but it happens. You end up fucking it up, you always do. You hate hurting them. When you know you're hurting them you try to end it, because fucking you can do but relationship stress, you can't do. You can't be monogamous. The family, the marriage, the white picket fence—it's not going to happen for you, and you've accepted that. You've tried relationships and you always end up cheating. It's better for all parties that there are no relationships involved. Like with Emmy. You've been trying to keep it casual sex but then she goes and says 'I love you' and you don't know what to say. Fucking you can do but love, you can't do.

You know from experience that what keeps them coming back isn't just the great sex, it's that little bit of yourself you drip feed to them, the loving, the care, the pure you. You're a warm, gentle person. You allude to the possibility that they could one day have more, and maybe they can, you're not sure—nothing's certain in life. So the women believe they could possibly have the mind-boggling sex and the deep, emotional relationship. Unfortunately, they don't know the pain it causes you when you release emotion. There isn't much more you can offer, that you can ever really offer. You know they only chase you and say they love you because you're unattainable.

There's no way you can be with Emmy, but you feel like you can tell her anything. You have too much dark in you, and just as much light, and so does she. The sexual chemistry is off the charts, and her heart is pure, but then she can be quite flippant and crazy, be hurtful and unpredictable. There have been times she's really hurt you, but that's sort of why you want her. You like her craziness, her light and her dark—all of it. She's opened up to you completely. She's too open. She'll learn the hard way, and you really feel for her sometimes. There have been so many times where she's sent you abusive messages that it's over but then she's apologising a week later, but she's already hurt you by that stage hasn't she?

She's like a ping-pong ball, and you could watch her go back and forth all day.

What a body! And a looker! You really hit the jackpot with her. A woman like that can't be kept, especially by you—who are *you*, anyway? If you ever let her in she would take one look around and say 'is that it?', and she'd be out the door, and then what? You're already falling for her, fall any harder and you'll be in danger territory. You're a player, that's who you are. If you were going to try the white picket fence it'd have to be with a woman you weren't head-over-heels about. You can't do love, you just can't do it. What you want is a house, a place of your own. You've never had that and that's what you want from life. You feel blessed that you're alive, and can function, and that you didn't kill yourself like your sister did with a drug overdose after the hard life you both had in that fucked-up, shit country town you won't mention. Religion, God, Heaven and Hell, the Catholic Church in your experience is the devil on Earth. That's why you're drawn to the ethnics, they don't have fucked up fake families like Aussies do.

You can't help it, one night you decide to tell Emmy everything. You're drunk, it's the only way you can tell her. You tell her about all the women, and about your sister, and the sexual abuse when you were both kids—just a fucking kid! But you don't harp on that shit, you've survived it, you fucking survived. You've got a job you enjoy, your music, and soon you will have a house. You're blessed, and you're not broken, despite what society might think. You've overcome the shit from the past, and you've got goals now, dreams and structure.

After you tell her you cry in her arms and then you make love to her. You stay the night with her. She's powdery soft, smooth and warm. You tell her you love her and you want to be with her—it's what you feel at the time, and the emotions are overflowing. But when the pain hits in the morning, you give her sweet kisses and leave, and as you're walking out the door you know you'll never see her again.

The following night you meet up with Lia, another girl you've been seeing on and off for a year, and you fuck her all night. Lia's keen on a relationship so you say okay. She's a bit detached and depressed, but she reminds you of your sister, and you know how to manoeuvre her, how to be with her. You're not head-over-heels but you know what's coming with her. Of course you'll still play, but not right now. You just want to focus on work and the Emmy thing really took it out of you. You tell Emmy you have a new girlfriend and it's over. Time for some work and stability. Emmy keeps texting, but eventually she'll get the message and stop. It's really the best for both of you. You're a player, it's what you are, and you know you were never good for each other. You're not sure exactly what you want out of life but you're sure she'll find her way. She's a strong cookie that one, she'll find herself a good bloke, one that can love her and treat her right.

13.

The Bridal Wars

Sometimes Tasha thinks her life is as dramatic as the Greek melodramas her parents are obsessed with. It doesn't surprise her. She *is* Greek after all. It's part of her heritage, her culture, for things to be so passionate, so intense. Tasha sips her tea while her mother gives her the backstory in Greek, because the episode playing is a repeat of yesterday.

'… the man was married, and then he went with her best friend, to do the business, and now she's pregnant, and the whole village know …'

Tasha can't be bothered using her brain. That's what work's for. She's *so* over work. If she has to sit through another marketing campaign she's going to lose it. She just wants Con to propose so she can get pregnant, have a baby, and never work again.

Tasha's dad is out so it's just the girls. Tasha's always been a mummy's girl. But this affection shouldn't be considered any kind of concurrence with her sister Olga's opinion of their father. Tasha's always been a staunch believer that her dad is an amazing dad, that he provided everything they needed, put food on the table, supported their education, and he never asked for a single dollar like Aussie families do even though he came to Australia with nothing. Her dad built the family home with his bare hands. It's walking distance to Mentone beach. So what if he hit them every now and then? It was the 90s. Everyone got hit.

Tasha checks the wall clock. It's three. And she still needs to vote, go home, and get ready before Con comes over. The wind outside is stressing her out. It's pulling at the trees the same way Tasha wants to yank at her cousin Betty's hair.

'Anyway ... what else is new?'

Her mum shrugs, sips her tea. '*Tipota.*' Nothing. Her gaze lands near Tasha's feet. 'Is that a new bag?'

Tasha combs her fingers through her long, brown hair. 'Oh—yep.'

'Another one? How many bags you going to buy? I count thirty bags in your room upstairs—thirty! And how many you have at your house?'

'That's why I work, Mum. So I can buy the things that I like.'

Her mother leans forward, lifts the red Birkin by the straps, rotates it this way and that. 'It's nice. How much? Two-hundred?'

Tasha shakes her head.

'If it's more than three hundred *ise belli.*'

Tasha snatches it from her clutch. 'I'm not stupid. Anyway, have you got any goss?'

Tasha's mum cosies back into the couch. '*Ti* goss? No goss.'

'Don't pretend with me. What's happening with the bridal wars? How is *Thia* Fotini?'

She sighs, the worry creasing her forehead. 'Not the best.'

'I don't blame her. Poor Leni.'

All their lives cousin Betty has been pulling shenanigans to get attention, but this time she's gone too far, this time she has *really* taken the cake, or the wedding cake, so to speak. Announcing her engagement only two weeks after their cousin Leni announced hers was by far her bitchiest move. The news had spread through the family grapevine like wildfire. Of course it was payback for Leni being brave enough to give Betty and her mum, *Thia* Dalida, a piece of her mind. Tasha had wished Betty *I ora I kali* when she saw her at a work function, she was courteous, even joyful, but Tasha was good at being fake when she needed to be and her allegiance was one hundred percent with Leni. Tasha despised working for the same company as Betty. She was convinced Betty followed her there just to copy her.

'Leni say she going to marry in Bali—Bali!—if she have to invite Betty so of course *Thia* Fotini ... she was crying to me on the phone yesterday "how can she have a wedding and not invite the family" and "what will everyone say, they will be so hurt", you know, all these things. It's very hard. I don't know how she's going to get through this.'

All Tasha could do was shake her head. 'I can't believe Leni has to give up on having a wedding because of them.'

'Tasha, they are both my sisters. Imagine how hard it is for me!'

'And what's gonna happen at Tim and Dina's wedding? Don't be surprised if *Thia* Dalida starts something, and you know how sensitive Leni is.'

'Don't worry. I spoke to *Thia* Androula and she said Dina made sure to not put *Thia* Fotini's family and *Thia* Dalida's family on same table and on different sides of the reception.'

'Good. I wonder where she'll put us ... anyway, it's not our problem, and you—' here Tasha points at her mum, 'stay out of it. We don't need any more headaches.'

'I will! I got my own problems.'

Tasha pauses. 'What problems?'

'I have to make sure everything is good with you and Con.'

'*Again,* Mum?'

'*Tasia,* you can't roam the streets with Con forever. You need to decide.'

'I'll decide when I'm ready.'

'You are not getting any younger—and I am getting older. I want to be finished with my children too. Sam is married, now it's your turn.'

'Why don't you put this kind of pressure on Olga?'

'Olga—with the help of God—she will find her way too.'

Her mum gets distracted by the television, turns up the volume using the remote. 'This is the movie I was telling you about. Look.'

Tasha finishes the last of her tea. 'I'm going.'

'You just got here!'

'I told you, I was just popping in. I gotta go. Love you.' Tasha plants a kiss on her confused mother's brow.

'Don't forget to vote!' she calls out after her.

Tasha drives to the town hall in her red sports car wearing seven hundred dollar Dior sunglasses that make her look *so* Kim Kardashian. Is it a crime to take pride in the way you look? Tasha didn't think so. She's worked hard for it. But lately, all the cool, trendy things she owns have done little to lessen her irritable mood. Usually buying things makes her feel better. She doesn't know why, but she doesn't want to examine why either. Or talk about it. She just hopes it's a phase she'll be over soon.

In the queue to vote, Tasha's Birkin handbag hangs from her forearm like a diamond bracelet. She catches a few guys checking her out. Let them, she thinks. They're only enjoying what they know they can't have. She tosses her hair to encourage it.

Tasha lifts her mobile from the back pocket of her designer jeans. Helena is calling, the oldest of the female cousins.

'I'm fine, just waiting in line to vote. How are you?'

'I voted already.'

'I don't give a shit, man. I've always just voted for who my dad votes for—lol.'

'Me too. Hey I just went to Leni's.'

'And?'

'She won't come out of her room. She's been crying for days. *Thia* Fotini is so stressed.'

Tasha sighs. 'Poor thing. But what can we do? Seriously. Nothing. Anyway, I'll see you at the wedding next week.'

'OMG, everyone's getting married. You're next! Then me.'

'Hopefully. Anyway, see you soon.'

The queue isn't moving fast enough for Tasha. Who runs the country isn't really an issue she has time for. Let them argue over it in parliament. The Australian government should really adopt the American system. Why should she be forced to vote?

When Tasha makes it to the front, she's handed a long polling form. At one of the cardboard booth partitions she puts a big number one in the box marked 'Tony Abbott, Liberal Party', then she chooses whatever for the rest of the numbers. Someone's got to stop all the boats, she thinks. That's what her dad's always saying. When were people going to learn that you can't just jump the queue in life? Just like her dad, you got to wait your turn.

When Tasha gets home she's exhausted. Maybe she's coming down with a cold. She thinks about the Skype session with Olga a few weeks ago. They talked for hours, about life, about everything. Tasha's still so angry at her for moving overseas. She's never been able to understand her sister, has never been able to wrap her head around Olga's thought processes.

Tasha slips off her shoes, lays on the couch, and takes a fifteen minute power nap. She knows she shouldn't, because she'll have trouble sleeping at night, but she seriously can't keep her eyes open.

At about five-thirty Tasha starts getting ready. She straightens any bits of hair that have become wavy since she washed and straightened it two days ago. Then she applies her makeup, chooses a sexy outfit: a tight, knee-length skirt, stiletto heels, and a fitted, long-sleeved, red cashmere top which she tucks into her skirt to draw attention to her waistline. Tasha likes to dress up for her man. It makes her feel like a woman.

Con is all polished up when he arrives, just like Tasha likes him to be. They go to their favourite restaurant down St Kilda beach, sip wine and chat. They are such a good-looking couple. They are one of those couples everyone wishes they were, and Tasha is sure the whole family will agree. Con is the first man she is introducing to her extended family. She has been planning it for a while, taking him to her cousin Tim's wedding as her official date. Once you introduce a guy then that's pretty much it. You only introduce if you're sure.

'You look really gorgeous tonight, babe.'

Tasha loves that. 'Thanks, babe. So do you.'

'It'll be cool meeting your family at the wedding.'

Tasha nods, takes another sip of her wine, drops her gaze ever so subtly. 'Yeah. Just don't expect it to go as smoothly as when I met all your family—lol.'

Con reaches across the table for her hand. She looks up at him. 'It'll be fine, don't stress, okay?'

Tasha nods.

Later they go back to Tasha's place and have hot sex. He makes her come twice. Tasha's glad she lasered every single one of the hairs. It's so much cleaner, not like her hippy sister Olga. Ew, disgusting. Hair is gross. Sometimes after sex Tasha wonders if her dad still thinks she's a virgin. But she knows it doesn't matter. Tasha's lucky. She can do whatever she likes. Times have changed, and Tasha *has* acknowledged that she and her brother Sam were not subjected to the same rules as Olga. But is that a reason to leave your boyfriend of five years and run off with your best friend to the UK declaring you're a lesbian? That seemed a bit extreme to Tasha. It was hard to tell who in the extended family knew and who didn't as it was a topic not to be mentioned, and Tasha's parents were dealing with it by pretending Olga never called a year ago from the UK to confess. They were still waiting for Olga to settle down with a good Greek boy. Secretly, Tasha hoped for the same.

Con doesn't stay the night. He's organised to go hunting for rabbits early the next day. Tasha's learned to live with his hobby. Her mum doesn't think it's a big deal. 'It's a man sport.'

Tasha goes straight to bed after Con leaves, tries to sleep. But she can't. She's always been a great sleeper but lately sleep has teased her the same way she would tease guys she wasn't interested in.

At ten-thirty, Tasha thinks fuck it, gets up, pours herself a glass of red and turns on the telly. She finds the Netflix documentary Olga bribed her two hundred dollars to watch. Tasha didn't care about the money, but if her sister wanted her to watch something that badly, best to put her out of her misery and watch it, Tasha thought.

A few minutes into the *The True Cost* Tasha is already muttering negative commentary. Why was Olga pretty much *forcing* her to watch some depressing documentary about how clothes are made? We are giving the poor countries jobs to make clothes for us. What's so wrong about that? Okay they don't make much money. Only three dollars a day. But their cost of living is cheaper so it works out. If they don't like sewing clothes they can get other jobs in worse conditions. Why should Tasha be made to feel bad for buying clothes?

Tasha endures, only because of the stupid promise—and seriously, if she had known that *this* was what she was going to be exposed to she would have not agreed. Yes it wasn't good all those people died in that garment factory but how was exposing someone like Tasha—an innocent consumer—to images of dead bodies, helping? Tasha didn't have the power to stop any of it from her couch in Melbourne.

The narrative continues, and maybe it's the wine, or her lucid state, but Tasha's mind begins to become entangled in the intricate ethical web of politics: *Fast Fashion. The way to solve the problems in your life is through consumption. Advertising. Happiness is based on stuff. Capitalism. Chemicals they spray the cotton with are giving people cancer. Genetically modified seeds. The company that makes seeds is the same company that makes pesticides and they also produce drugs to treat cancer. In the last sixteen years there have been 250,000 farmer suicides. Largest reported wave of farmer suicides in history. The workers get beaten if they complain about the working conditions. A woman crying. She says 'if you buy our clothes you have our blood on your hands'.*

She was born in Bangladesh. She has never lived outside Bangladesh so all she knows is Bangladesh. She has no means to leave. She lives near the garment factory where she works. She has a small room in a house she shares with other garment workers. She was born a garment worker and she will die a garment worker. She has been boxed in by her destiny: the nameless garment worker. But she has a name. Jaya. Jaya has long brown hair she likes to tie in a bun. Jaya likes to look her best even though she only owns three dresses. Jaya will, from time to time, laugh with the other girls she lives with, but she hates the conversations where they talk themselves into hope and end up exhausted and quiet. Jaya cries on most nights for her daughter who lives two days away from Jaya with her parents. Her daughter must live with her parents because Jaya has nowhere to leave her when she goes to work. Jaya must work. If she does not work she will not earn the three dollars a day she needs to buy food for her family. Jaya's drinking

water is a river near the factory. The factory pumps its chemical waste into the water, tonnes and tonnes of frothy, dirty waste. Jaya uses this water to bathe too. She bathes with a large bucket she carries from the river to her house. Many people become sick from the water but Jaya has no choice, she must drink from this water because there is no other water for miles, and that water is also polluted. Jaya sometimes wishes the human body did not need food or water to survive.

Jaya sews with her mask on. She will sew for fourteen hours with only a short lunch break. When there is a deadline on an order and the bosses yell to hurry, Jaya's hands tremble. Jaya knows that the bosses have their bosses in western countries and they won't pay her bosses if the work is not done and then Jaya won't get paid either. Jaya feels dizzy when she sews. There is a chemical swirl in her head. Sometimes she is so dizzy her head drops but the boss is there to yell. Jaya's body hurts. Her back, her wrists, her legs—it all hurts, always. There are bars on the windows. The room is hot and Jaya can't breathe in a full inhalation because when she does her chest hurts and she coughs, she coughs the chemicals. The air is like evaporated methylated spirits and bleach. There are 2000 workers in her factory, all sewing, all thinking. While she sews she thinks of her best friend, Bati, who died in the factory fire a few streets away. Jaya has not allowed her mind to process that she will never see Bati again, that they will not walk to the river again together, or talk about dreams they knew would never come.

The wall to Jaya's right shifts, startles her. It's loud enough to be heard over the chorus of sewing machines. Many stop but they are quickly barked at by the bosses. The women bow their heads, continue. They do this because last week two women complained and the bosses beat them with sticks and scissors and punched them and the women were taken away and nobody has seen them since. Jaya's heart is beating fast. She knows she may die here. She has visions all the time, that the walls cave in on her. Everyone dies, she knows this, but she doesn't want to die in here, in this building, where she is imprisoned by her destiny, where she is a slave to the wealthy women of the west who wear the beautiful clothes she makes with her blood and the blood of her friends and the blood of her country. Jaya has an image in her mind of what these women look like. She has an image of one woman. This woman, she calls her Tasha. Jaya and Tasha are the same age, although Tasha did not have a man rape her, and Tasha eats meals three times a day, and has clean water from the springs, and Jaya wonders sometimes, if Tasha, when she puts on a dress that Jaya has made, she wonders if Tasha thinks of Jaya. Does Tasha think that in order to make her dress, Jaya's uncle committed suicide because he had no money to pay the seed companies what he owed for the pesticides? Does she think of the pain Jaya suffers to make her clothes, so she can wear her clothes, the many, many clothes she has? When Tasha notices that part of the hem is unstitched, does she get angry that the garment is faulty, or does she think of the tremble in Jaya's hands which caused the fabric in the sewing machine to run off course because the wall beside her had moved again and the sound was like an earthquake? Jaya heard that women like Tasha have enough clothes to dress one village. Jaya is thirsty as she sews. She begins to cry. She thinks of Tasha drinking water from a clear glass. Clear water in a clear glass, a luxury Jaya only dreams of. Jaya hates Tasha. She hates her. Jaya thinks: my life is a long piece of thread. I take the thread and I sew. My life is a dress. A dress I'll never wear. I dress the rich with my blood. My tears cleanse the dress before it is shipped to Tasha.

Tasha wakes from her dream coughing.

A week later, on the day of the wedding, Con is dressed to impress, but he is speechless when he turns up at Tasha's and she answers the door in her pyjamas.

'What's wrong, Tasha? Are you okay?'

Tasha doesn't know how to answer the question so she says, 'yeah, fine, I'm just running a bit late. We'll be okay.'

He looks at his watch. 'The wedding's at three and it's two. Have I got the times mixed up?'

'No, no—it's just … um …'

He brings her into his arms and holds her. But she can't relax. She subtly wiggles her way out.

'What is it, babe? You're really starting to freak me out.'

'It's just … I …' She looks into his eyes. 'I don't think you should come.'

Con blinks at her words. 'Wh…hat? And you tell me this *now*? Is that why you didn't want to catch up this week? You said you weren't feeling well, were you *lying* to me?'

Tasha is taken aback by his escalating anger. It triggers things in her. 'Can you not speak to me like that please? I'm sorry … I'm just not ready for you to meet my family.'

'You've met *my* family. Tasha, I love you. We love each other! This is serious for me. I want a future with you. I told you, babe. Why are you doing this?'

'I don't know,' she trembles. One tear falls and she catches it quickly. 'I don't fucking know.'

'I think you do fucking know.'

Tasha looks at the tiles on the floor and holds her breath. He takes a few steps back, then he punches the wall with his fist. Tasha jumps, but her gaze stays fixed. She doesn't see him walk out. The door slams. She exhales.

Oh the drama of it, it's like a theatre production, the photography, the lighting, the audience, the stage, the music. The romantic ambiance. All perfectly rehearsed and timed, the final film to be edited into a one-hour version of perfection, a blue-print for the married couple's lifetime together. The invitations match the baby pink colour scheme. Candles and flowers handpicked by the designers to bring a certain softness to this very special, elaborate event, a celebration of the lifelong struggle to find that special someone to complete this picturesque photograph. The bridesmaids gleam, bestowed with the honour of such a role, of being cast in the wedding production. The costumes, oh the costumes—bridesmaids, mother-of-the-bride—made of the very best fabrics, imported handmade Thai silk. And the bridal gown, diamond-encrusted ivory silk, adorned with lace appliqué, draped in a luscious, soft, silk organza veil. You can hear the sighs of every woman in attendance in awe of the bride and groom waltzing on the dancefloor to Celine Dion and the sounds of destiny, wishing they could be the bride in *this* story, and every married woman is re-living her wedding day, wishing she could somehow turn back the Cinderella clock, replay the fairytale instead of being stuck, in some sort of alternate reality.

And then there's Tasha, who did make it on time to the church ceremony (just), but she wasn't as polished as expected, so she attracted a bit of 'are you okay?' and 'you don't seem yourself today' just before the confetti was thrown and blown away by the wind. But Tasha just smiled and reassured.

'Where's Con?' Helena asked.

'He's not feeling well.'

'Oh, that's a shame.'

Did Helena believe her? Tasha wasn't sure.

'Hey, where's Con?' her cousin Irine asked as they queued to enter the grand ballroom, her four-year-old son hanging from her like a circus acrobatic. 'You told me he was coming—or have I lost my mind? I think I've lost my mind since having George.'

'You're fine. He's come down with a flu and didn't want to give it to anyone.'

'Oh, poor thing. Tell him I hope he gets better soon.'

And then her mum. 'Where's Con? I told everyone you will bring him and now he is not here. What happened?'

'He's sick.'

Tasha's mum looked her up and down. 'Are you saying the truth?'

Tasha smiled. 'Of course.'

Tasha is participating in conversation at the table with her cousins, but only on its fringes. There's beer, wine, soft drinks and plenty of Greek dips to go round. Her brother Sam and his wife Dijana are at a different table, too preoccupied with her nieces to notice Tasha's hair is out of place—i.e. there are wavy bits. And she doesn't have as much foundation on her face—did she even remember to put foundation on? Was everyone looking at her? Was she losing her mind?

Leni is at Tasha's table with her fiancé, Tim, and everyone's laughing and trying to keep her spirits propped up. And across the reception are the rest of Tasha's cousins, sitting with Betty, just as her mum said they would be. Everything's been arranged, sorted, scripted like a play. There are two hundred people in the reception, people Tasha doesn't know well but recognises from past events like weddings, funerals, christenings. Next to Tasha is Con's empty chair. Tasha's not sure if she cares. She just feels numb. But she *should* care. Shouldn't she care more that he shouts at her like that? Is that why she told him not to come? Why *did* she tell him not to come?

Leni and Tim leave the table, and only a few short minutes later *Thia* Dalida arrives to say hello, bathing in the glory as everyone adorns her with congratulations on Betty's engagement. Tasha doesn't engage with Helena's 'look who's here now that Leni's not at the table' non-verbal gossipy eye communication like she usually does.

'And next is Tasha!' *Thia* Dalida says.

All her cousins agree with glee.

'Hopefully!' Tasha enthuses.

'Sorry to hear your boyfriend no here,' *Thia* Dalida continues. 'I hope he is okay?'

'He's just sick.'

'No worry! We meet him another day!'

Everyone laughs. Is this a horror film, Tasha thinks. It feels like a horror film.

When *Thia* Dalida leaves, Helena asks Tasha if she's okay.

'Yeah, I'm fine. I'm just gonna go to the bathroom.'

'I'll come.'

On their way Helena talks under her breath about the whole bridal wars saga, and she's saying all this stuff that Tasha would ordinarily be very interested in, but Tasha cannot seem to process any of it so she just nods and agrees.

Helena pushes open the heavy bathroom door. The room is fancy, decked out in marble with floor to ceiling mirrors, organic hand soaps, perfumes and moisturises. Leni and Betty are washing their hands, both pretending that the other isn't there. Helena and Tasha stop.

'Hi girls,' Helena says.

'Hi,' Betty enthuses. 'Having fun?'

'I'm not sure …' Tasha says.

Nobody takes any note of this. Betty pulls some paper towel to dry her hands. 'Helena, you haven't seen my ring yet.'

'Let me look!'

Betty presents it to them. Helena nods in admiration. 'Beautiful.'

'I know.'

Leni snorts. It's a soft snort, but loud enough for all to hear. Betty narrows her eyes at Leni. 'Do you have a problem?'

'Why would I have a problem?'

Betty rolls her eyes. Then they both go to exit and accidentally slam into each other.

'Watch it!' Leni says.

'You fucking watch it,' Betty retaliates.

They start to push each other.

'Girls!' Helena says.

A larger woman pushes the door open and stops. They all watch her proceed to the cubicle then the girls reignite in combat.

'This is completely embarrassing, girls,' Helena hisses. 'Pull yourselves together.'

But they won't, so Helena does something nobody has ever seen her do—she grabs them both by the hair.

'Ouch, ow, ow,' they both cry, and she pulls them like that, out of the bathroom and out of the reception centre, around the corner to the carpark, and by this stage—probably because other cousins have seen this—the rest of the cousins are gathering in the carpark, including cousin Thanos, with pita bread and tzatziki, like he's brought snacks to a soccer match to better enjoy the entertainment. Tasha follows the commotion, dumbfounded.

Helena releases the girls, begins her stern lecture but she's quickly cut off by the girls who start ripping into each other, pulling hair, wrestling, and all the cousins are trying to reason with them, but there's so much rage, accumulated rage, years and years of rage, snowballed rage from all their parents, and their parents' parents, and all the ancestors, generations and generations of rage. All the cousins are affected, debating on who is right and who is wrong. But Tasha isn't saying anything at all.

'You've always been jealous of me since the day I was born,' Leni yells. 'Always getting your mum to do all your dirty work because you're a sook, a weak sook!'

'That's because you're a cruel selfish bitch!'

Leni yanks herself from Betty's clutches. 'Selfish? Why? Because I have a life and I don't want you in it? I don't have to invite you to my parties. You're a trouble-maker, and you gossip about people—and every time I do something you don't like, you get your mum to tell my mum off. You bully my family! And we can't say anything because we're "family"! Don't you get it? I want you out of my life!'

They stop. Everyone stops. The girls are panting. The cousins are delirious. Nobody knows what the hell is going on but Tasha, Tasha, something happens to Tasha, deep inside. Olga's words, which didn't seem relevant a few weeks ago, suddenly click into some part of her brain's logic. *You don't have to subscribe to it.* Tasha wants to speak. She doesn't know what she wants to say but when she opens her mouth the words glide out, like they are her destiny:

'Girls, can I say something? Women on the other side of the planet, died to make your clothes. They were forced to make your clothes. They should let the boats come. Weddings are fucked. Grow up!'

And now it's everyone else's turn to look dumbfounded. They just stare at Tasha, like *did Tasha just say that? Am I dreaming?* And just like that, Tasha feels better. So she nods, turns on her heel. And she leaves the wedding.

13.

The Wog Chick At The Laneway Gig

There is only one reason, and one reason alone, that I left him. He wasn't abusive. He wasn't violent. In fact, he was a good husband. He worked. I stayed home with the kids. He was just boring, that's all. Drop dead boring. So boring I wanted to kill myself. People were like 'why are you leaving him? Did he hit you? He's such good guy'. They couldn't fit the concept in their heads. Why? Why? Why?

He did try though. I dragged him to a rock music gig once. It was my first one too. I can't believe my first gig was at the age of twenty-nine. It was pretty timid music. It wasn't heavy metal or anything. But I was the only conservative wog mum in a mosh pit of Aussie rockers, with my cardigan and long proper skirt. He was complaining the music was too loud. I found a seat for him down the back. Then I went all the way to the front, where the music was at its loudest, and stood there. The music electrified my soul. Electrocuted it. It's what I needed. He sat there with his arms folded all night. I let him.

Music became my addiction. I got pink streaks in my long, brown hair. I started dressing differently, more sexy. Wilder. I'd look up gigs on the internet and go. He wouldn't complain because he didn't want to go. I had no friends to go with because the only friends I had were his friends and they were all like him. So I just went on my own. I didn't care anymore.

Something I discovered quite quickly is that despite what the wogs think, there is nothing wrong with going somewhere on your own.

It's nice not having to rely on others. You can just go out whenever you like. It's lonely sometimes, but then you might meet someone and who knows where that might lead? I couldn't believe I spent my young adult years at techno clubs. My parents were so freaked out by Aussie pubs. *They're dangerous*, they would say. *Full of Australian drunks. Stick to your own kind. Be wary of strangers.* I believed them. Little did I know that pubs were where I belonged!

I told all the wogs to go to hell. Got my own place. It was the first time I lived on my own. My turn for fun now. I have the kids on the weekdays, he has them on weekends. I work from home as a beautician so it works out plus he pays me child support and I get some government benefits. Every Friday and Saturday night, I'm out. I go to pubs and rock venues where the music is so loud it screams for you. I stay out until past that time of night where it feels wrong to still be out.

I started off not knowing anyone. I'd go to The Tote down Collingwood where the Aussies congregate. I'd sit and watch them. So cool and laid back. I idolised the indie musos, studied the way they played their instruments.

Pony on Collins Street was where I met Sam. He works behind the bar. Pony is so authentically rock. Sticky, dirty, dark. You can't sit on the toilet seat—it's so disgusting—you have to pee standing up which is why there's pee all over the floor. Pony is where the bad-arse music goes down. Ripped corduroy couches, layers of posters plastered on the walls. Pony is the kind of bar that would give both my parents a heart attack. Lucky for me I don't see them much. I just want to be free, listen to music, and have sex. Not procedural, obligatory sex, but really good—bad sex.

Sam had just got off work and was having a drink when we met. We were both sitting on the couch in the downstairs bar. The night was winding down and most people were gone. I was drinking my soft drink, and he looked interesting, so I just started talking to him. 'I'm Viv,' I said. 'Vivien, Viv for short.'

'Hey, Viv, I'm Sam.'

We got chatting and I told him about my situation.

Sam is tall, lanky and aloof, and he seems to operate on some other realm completely separate from planet earth. We became friends on Facebook straight away and he said we could hang out no problem. The ten year age gap—which is mindboggling when I think about it—is irrelevant, because it feels like we're the same age even though he's younger. He's a muso (too cool), plays drums, and he's invited me to some of his gigs and introduced me to some of his friends. All Aussies of course. I'm not gonna lie, it is a bit awkward, being the only wog chick. Sometimes it feels like I'm a bit of a tag along but I'm getting used to it.

It didn't take long for me to fall for Sam. He's so thoughtful, sends me music links through Facebook to expand my repertoire. He has really adorable qualities that have me thinking about him day and night. Like when I talk to him, he looks at me like he's completely absorbed by what I'm saying, yet it's clearly evident he disappears briefly into the library of his mind at points during the conversation, and then when he seeks clarification, and I bring him up to speed, he says 'oh, right, yeah' in this endearing adorable way.

It's late, we're at Pony and Sam's annoyed with me because I'm drunk. Alcohol doesn't agree with me. I can get drunk on two drinks.

'That's what I love about you, Viv,' he says, and he's blind drunk. 'I love that you don't drink. I wish I was like you.'

'No you don't. I feel so uptight. Like I want to be free and I don't know how. But you're free, you're really free.'

Sam takes his phone out, starts texting. Then, surprisingly confident, I begin to run my fingertip up and down his leg, up and down, up and down. He continues to message, pretends like I'm not doing what I'm doing.

'Great, Viv, now I've got to go—I don't want to leave you like this.'

'I'll be fiiiinnne.'

'You don't seem fine—and I've got to wait for my ride outside.'

'I'll come out with you.'

Outside it's bitter cold. It's the kind of cold that makes you want to pack up everything and move to Greece forever. He lights up a smoke. I stand next to him to get my nicotine fix. I've never smoked either.

'When was the last time you had a drink?' he asks.

'Oh … I don't knowww …'

'You don't know?'

'Nooo.'

'Why?'

'I don't know …'

'But why don't you drink? Is there a reason?'

'I don't know.'

'You don't know?'

'Nooo—let's meet for coffee?'

'I'll see you next week,' he says.

'Nooo, I want coffee … why won't you meet me for coffee?'

'Because I'm seeing you next week.'

'You're mad that I had a drink.'

'No, I'm just worried—are you gonna be okay to drive?'

'Well if you're worried, come with me.'

'No, I've got stuff to do.'

'Like what?'

'Stuff.'

'Okay then, Mr Stuff, I'm going.' So I turn away, down Little Collins Street, away from him, down and down and away. He calls after me. I keep going.

Months pass and my feelings for Sam intensify. It's like I'm going to burst. I have wasted so much of my life not doing and saying what I want. Life is too short not to tell people how you feel. I am going to tell Sam. I'm just going to come right out and say it. I just have to find the right time.

Larry and Alicia are my two new friends. I met Alicia when she came to my place for a wax and we hit it off and I met Larry through her. Larry isn't into punk rock at all. He's twenty-one, wears jazzy suits and hats, looks like he's just stepped out of a 50s Hollywood murder mystery. Alicia is so hot she makes me question if I am bi-sexual. Not that I've ever kissed a girl but you never know. She has long, blonde hair, bright blue eyes, and a smile that'd calm anyone down. She's recently moved to Melbourne to work on her career as a singer-songwriter. I take them to one of Sam's gigs to get their opinion.

'I saw the way he looked at you, darling,' Alicia said the next day on the phone. 'He adores you, he looks up to you.'

'At the very least you know you have a good friend in him, and that's what counts,' Larry said on the phone after Alicia.

Life is about timing. I have to wait for the right time.

Two weeks later, it's a Saturday morning and I'm at home scrolling through my Facebook feed. My ex has just picked up the kids and there's a gaping hole in my chest. I'm so bored of my existence. I feel like crying but no tears come out. The loneliness is creeping towards me like two hundreds spiders. I only have ten friends on Facebook. I deleted everyone I knew after I left him. Didn't need any more feeling like I'm not normal from family and extended family. No thanks. Anyway, I'm scrolling, and that's when I see Sam's band is playing a gig this afternoon. The theme is 90s covers. Why didn't he invite me? I really need to get out.

I text him. *Hey, Sam, what's this gig in the afternoon?*

Nothing special, but come along if you want.

Rad, see you there.

Alicia's working but Larry is home today. I text him to come along.

I'll see.

Today is the day. I can feel it. I'm going to tell him today.

I re-check the event. I haven't heard of the venue before but it's in Brunswick. I don't recognise any of the people who have said they're coming. I do feel a bit weird going, but I need to push through the weirdness. It's just my wog mentality making me doubt myself. There's nothing wrong with going out on your own. Nothing at all.

I turn my car down a street in Brunswick that ends in a carpark and the train tracks. There are hipsters and punks everywhere, I panic for a second, struggle for my breath, like when I wake in the crux of the night and the emptiness has a firm grip around my neck. This is a mistake. I don't fit in here. It's all Aussies, I don't fit.

The gig is in someone's shed that backs onto a laneway.

I park, turn the ignition off and text Larry: *It's in a shed.*

I push myself out of the car. It's cold and I'm under dressed. A train rushes past. There are guys with tattoos and spiky hair, girls with short skirts and fishnets, pink and red hair. Their outfits are so much hipper than mine. Everyone looks so much younger than me. The scent of pot wafts about the place, reminds me of my nightclubbing days at Metro or Greek nights at Billboards. Not that I ever touched the stuff. Not me, the good Cypriot girl.

My mobile beeps. I scramble for the company of a message.

It's Larry: *Hahhahahhahh … have fun! Hahhahhahah.*

Ha, Ha, I laugh, dryly, in my head.

I spot Sam in the crowd drinking. I go over to him.

'Why didn't you tell me it was in a shed?' I playfully slap his shoulder.

He grins. 'You didn't ask.'

The shed is set up like a music venue with a makeshift stage in the corner. Each band plays a thirty minute set of songs by famous bands, and while the next band sets up, a DJ plays in the opposite corner. It's a tight squeeze. There's moshing and madness. It's over-the-top loud. I jump up and down a little on the periphery. I don't know the lyrics to any of the songs but it's like I'm the only one who doesn't.

I want to be absorbed into the moment, to belong to it, to them, but I can't, I don't. Are they looking at me, judging me, wondering who I am? Cypriot girls my age don't hang out in sheds. They are at home looking after the kids, cooking dinner for their husband, fantasising about the life they could have had but were too afraid to pursue.

Fuck that. No way am I ever going to be with a wog guy again. They are all mummy's boys and just want a wife for the sake of having one. I need an Aussie bloke, a guy without a drop of culture.

When Sam's band starts setting up, I sit on the torn couch beside him while he warms up on the drums. As I watch him my Dad's voice shouts in my mind: *Na min trepese*! You should be ashamed of yourself! I imagine him catching me in the shed, the look of disgust, enough to send him to the hospital. It wouldn't make a difference if I said that Sam invited me, and that he's a friend. To Dad, the word 'friend' always translated to 'boyfriend'. There was no in-between.

Sam is my first male friend.

'Yoo can no be friend wid man,' Mum would say. 'Man, he has thing, and his mind, is only on da thing.'

The sound of Sam's band jolts me out of suffocating wog land and into Aussie reality. It electrifies my senses, expands my mind. As they play, it's like I exist within the music and nowhere else.

After their set ends, and the next band is setting up, Sam is guzzling more booze. He heads out to the carpark with a bunch of his mates and I follow, unsure of what to do with myself. If only I were a boozer, a drinker, because then I'd be more relaxed, and then I could just meld into their group and mentality. But I don't feel like drinking. I hate the way alcohol makes me feel.

I stand next to Sam as he smokes to get my nicotine fix. We start talking about random stuff and somewhere in there I mention my parents, and them catching me here, and then we get onto the topic of marriage and previous loves. He says he still loves his ex-girlfriend who he broke up with a year ago.

'She's one of the most amazing women I have ever known.'

'How long were you together?'

'Two years.'

'Oh. Do you think it's salvageable?'

'Nah, we're too different.'

I explain that my ex-husband rescued me from a destructive family dynamic.

'That's fucked,' he says.

His words grate at my core. Fucked? I want to punch him. I want to tell him that if my ex hadn't done that I'd be dead. I would have slashed my wrists and they would have found me in the gutter. Fucked? Sam has no idea what fucked is, in his free Aussie life. He has no idea what cultural entrapment is. He thinks pining over an ex-girlfriend, who *he* broke up with, is pain. He should step into the wog bubble for some real pain.

'Not fucked,' I say directly into his eyes. 'Necessary.'

A few of his drunk friends stumble into our space. The sun has almost disappeared behind a grey haze and the crowd is getting rowdier, more annoying. I leave Sam, go into the shed and sit on the couches next to two other drunk or high people. I check my phone. No messages.

The bands play and play. It's darker now, the light has faded. I am tired. I want my bed and my kids. I return to Sam and his friends, mingle my way in, but I just want the night over. I can't carry my feelings anymore, I'm too exhausted by them. I just want to tell Sam how I feel and have it over with.

'Did you want to go and get a bite to eat after this?' I ask Sam out of nowhere. I wish I was high, I wish I had an excuse for what I'm about to do.

'Nah … I'm delirious … really, I'm so drunk I'm delirious.'

'Let's head off,' one of his male friends announces.

'Back to Sam's?' one of his female friends adds.

'Food,' another guy adds.

They all start walking away except Sam.

'We're gonna head off. Catch you at Pony soon, yeah?'

Where's my invitation? Its absence stabs at my ego. How can Sam be so rude? Or so drunk that he doesn't realise he's being rude? How can he leave me here with a shed-full of strangers and not care?

'Yeah, see ya.'

He turns away, begins to walk, is halfway down the laneway, but I just want this over with, I want all of this, over with. So I go up to him, all the way, tap him on the shoulder.

'Sam, can I talk to you for a minute? In private?'

'Yeah, sure.'

I lead him away from the group.

'What's up?'

I can't look him in the eyes. He's so tall. I look up and over his shoulder, up at the navy-blue sky for answers, hope. 'I have to tell you something but it's hard.'

'Come on, just say it,' he says, like he knows what's coming and wants it over with.

'Do you ever think of us as more than friends?' I force out.

'No ... no I don't ...' He drops his words into the cool Aussie air and then silence, each word falling to my skin to be absorbed, like misty rain drifting from a night sky. There's no validation of our friendship, no 'I think you're great'. Nothing.

'Thanks for letting me know,' comes out some time later.

'Cool, no problem,' and more silence on his part.

'We'll still be friends, yeah?'

'Yeah, sure. Hey my friends are waiting. I gotta go.'

'Oh, yeah, cool, well thanks.'

He hesitates, then pulls me in for a hug, a proper one, our first proper hug. 'Catch you soon,' he says.

'Yeah ...'

He turns away to re-join his pack, upholding his I'm-so-cool-I'm-a-pissed-muso image. They continue down the laneway, leaning on each other, rowdy girls and boys going back to his place to drink more, smoke pot, do stuff I know isn't good for me but want to do anyway. Stuff I missed out on.

I walk back to my car, get in. I burst into tears.

14.

The Fuck Buddy

Penny was going to find love this year and nothing was going to stop her. She had put her intention out to the universe and she was sure the universe would bring her gifts. She had planned it out like a project. In two years, she would be married. All she needed to do was apply and retain the same focus to finding a man as she did to her accounting career. She had achieved success in that part of her life, so there was no reason she couldn't achieve the same level of success in her love life. Penny and her father may have not seen eye-to-eye on many things in her life, but he was right when he said, *you can achieve anything in life with hard work*. He came to Australia with nothing and now he had so much.

But Penny didn't want just any kind of love. She wasn't going to accept anything less than love that ticked all the boxes. He'd have to be good looking, clean, handsome. Have a well-paid job, be focused on his career but not obsessed to the point where he ignored his wife. Penny wasn't going to settle for anything less than 'ridiculously in love'. He would have to be proactive, plan dinners and trips away, have his own home, or at least have a plan to buy a house if he was still living with his parents. He would definitely have to be a family man, but not too much of a family man that he would put his mother before his wife. Penny knew this would be a challenge as all Greek men were mummy's boys, yet Penny only really wanted to be with a Greek man. They would understand each other culturally, and there wouldn't be all the drama that comes with mixed race couples such as what religion they would baptise their children. Texts and phone calls every day were a must. No way was she going to do any of the chasing—that's a guy's job.

She hoped they would also have good sex. Penny had only ever had one other boyfriend, Stavro, and she wasn't sure, but she was pretty sure, she'd never felt the pleasure she was supposed to feel during the act. She'd never told anyone this though. Penny just didn't feel comfortable talking about such inappropriate things. The sex had been pleasant with Stavro, but when she was climbing to some sort of pinnacle she would always get to a point where she couldn't go any further, like she had hit some sort of invisible wall, and the only way she could progress further, was with the aid of her hand, and only if she imagined degrading scenarios that horrified her and made her feel dirty afterwards. Penny had only ever wanted to have sex with one man: her husband. She thought Stavros was the one. They waited one year before they were intimate just to make sure. But Penny was wrong. She wasn't going to make that same mistake. One other man before your husband was not as bad as some other women.

But at the age of thirty-eight, time was running out for Penny. She wanted a family. She was tired of sympathetic conversations with friends and family on her lack of finding a husband. She was tired of getting dressed up and going clubbing only to return home with no prospects. It wasn't *her fault* that all the men out there were idiots. Sure guys asked her out, but they were all duds. They didn't tick all her boxes, not even three-quarters of all her boxes, so what was the point? No, Penny was going to adopt a new strategy. She had whispered it to herself on New Year's Eve. It was her resolution. She was going to do something she had never done before. If she could find a husband then she would finally be able to move out of home and start her own life.

'I'm going to do it,' Penny said.

'Well everyone's doing it,' Peter said. 'I swear I just want to die sometimes when my mates tell me what they're doing. They've got two or three girls on the side they bang regularly—and I'm just here, stuck, with my mortgage, and the kids, and the wife. Life sucks.'

'Shh! I'm not going online to have sex, idiot. I want to find a good guy.'

Peter's tongue lacked the filter one might expect from a Greek and he had been accused of gossiping like a girl since their university days, so Penny always took his commentary with a grain of salt. Penny and her brother-in-law were always getting into taboo conversations. This conversation was a landmine though—if someone stumbled over it there'd be an explosion.

Conservatism, proper Greek behaviour, religion and ethics grew on the fruit trees at her parents' house where she still lived; hung on the tomato plants, ripe. Peter's two little girls were running around the backyard, picking fruit from the trees. The rest of Penny's family were around too, oohing and aahing and clapping with each discovery. Penny's father and brother chatted and smoked while supervising the bbq. Penny was the eldest of the three siblings yet both her siblings had made it to the altar before Penny, which was completely out of order and illogical in their culture.

'There's no harm in having a bit of fun while you're waiting for Mr Right.'

'Peter, don't you know me? You've known me for, what, 20 years? Seriously.'

'Like a *fuck buddy.*' He whispered the words, practically mouthed the words.

'Shh!' Penny was insulted by his use of the phrase. But it enthralled her too. It made Penny wonder how much sex Peter had before he married Roula, if any at all.

'I don't know how some girls do it,' Penny said. 'They must be on drugs or something.'

'Well believe me, some girls can do it, and do. Like on dating websites. People sign up and specify that they're only looking for sex.'

'That's because some people are weird,' she said matter-of-factly.

'Peter, you better not be saying anything stupid over there,' Roula called out from across the yard.

Penny punched Peter's arm.

What Penny didn't tell Peter was that she had already started chatting to a guy online. Rick and Penny had been chatting for a week when Rick told her he was online just for sex and did Penny want to meet him and fuck. Penny was outraged.

'Maybe we meet and we fall in love,' she threw back.

'Look, I'm a nice, honest guy,' Rick had said. 'But I have my reasons for not wanting to get involved emotionally with anyone on the website.'

Penny and Rick had agreed not to meet but to continue to chat online. Penny was surprised she had even agreed to *that*. But there was something about Rick's blatant honesty that made her curious to know more.

'Nothing wrong with having sex if both parties agree,' Peter added.

'I need an intellectual connection.'

'But it could be really liberating for you. I mean, don't you ever want some guy to just grab you and fuck you, like just take you and fuck you hard, no feelings, just fucking?'

Penny had never considered it before. I mean, sure, her fantasies were full of such experiences, and far worse. But they were just fantasies. Fantasies were not reality.

Penny and Chris had been messaging each other for a few days through the website, and Penny was happy to keep things that way for now. He didn't specify on his profile if he was Greek when she had stumbled across it while scrolling through a torrent of hideous-looking males. But his dark, Mediterranean features made it a good chance. He was half-smiling, not facing the camera directly. So she sent him a 'hello' and they picked up from there. She was right. He was Greek.

Chris owned his own photography business. He was four years older than her. Their dialogue was flirty, witty and intelligent. It filled those lonely night hours where there was nothing to do and she craved male attention.

But then lunch with her friend and work colleague, Clare, had her second guessing.

'Meet him as soon as possible.'

'But why? I want to get to know him first.'

'Oh, honey ...' Clare reached across the table and took Penny's hand. 'No. Because then you invest all this time and then you meet and there's no chemistry and then what? You've invested and it's amounted to nothing.'

'But intelligence is just as big a turn on for me.'

'Trust me, honey. I've met up with so many guys from those websites. Meet up. No chemistry? Nip it in the bud, immediately.'

Was Clare right? The sex guy, Rick, would regularly meet random girls and sleep with them—and effortlessly, or so he said—with no concern for chemistry or intellectual connection. Rick had raised an interesting point with Penny while they were chatting online one night. He said sex meant different things to different people. To him, it was like a sport.

'It's like masturbating but instead, wouldn't you like a hot guy to come and fuck you?'

'Really? Sport?'

'Yes.'

It surprised Penny that Rick not only confronted her, but also turned her on.

But of course, as friends do, Greta had a different opinion to Clare. 'Get yourself off that fucking website. It's addictive, a procrastinator's dream. Spend more time getting to know yourself, and the right man will come along in his own time.'

But Penny still went online. One night after her parents had gone to bed she was chatting with Chris.

'How come I can't see your face in your picture, NotSureAboutThis?' Chris messaged.

Penny was sitting with her legs outstretched on her bed, her laptop on her lap. Her bedroom door was closed and her parents were in their room downstairs. 'Because I'm not sure about all this!'

'But how am I supposed to know if I like what I see?'

'I assure you, you won't be disappointed.'

'Is that so?'

'Yes. It is.'

The conversation was enough to cause Penny to place the laptop on the floor, throw herself on her bed, slide her hand down her underwear and imagine. Penny was never into vibrators and always used her hand. She could only do it on her stomach. She could never orgasm on her back.

As Penny touched herself, memories of the time her mum caught her touching herself violated her mind. She was twelve and her mum yelled that she would go to hell for touching herself. She remembered how her mum took her straight to the Orthodox priest for confession, and how embarrassed she was confessing on her knees in front of the priest. After that incident she only masturbated when her parents were out, or when she knew they were fast sleep. Even at this age, Penny could not watch kissing or sex on TV in front of her parents, which was why one of the first things she did when she got a full-time job was buy a TV for her room. But she would still have to lower the volume to almost nothing when sex was playing.

Penny pushed the disturbing moments to the far reaches of her mind and returned Chris to the forefront. She imagined him touching her between her legs, kissing her thighs, entering her. She thought of him being rough, dominating and controlling, played out different scenarios, and she came not once, not twice, but three times.

After napping for a few minutes, Penny rose, hue cheeked, washed her hands then returned to the computer. His message was waiting for her: 'Well hopefully we will get to put that to the test.'

Penny checked if he was still online. He was. She sent through 'maybe' then clicked through to the tab 'personality tests' on his profile. Penny wasn't sure how these tests could possibly be accurate but curiosity had her examining more closely. Chris's test revealed he was 'The Bachelor'. He was also found to be 90% slutty in the slut test. The description attached to the results stated that he has the kindest of intentions, is considerate and affectionate, but the moment he senses a woman is wanting more than something casual, he is quick to explain, with sincerity, that he isn't looking for anything serious and is onto the next girl. Penny decided to take a test of her own. After clicking through a series of twenty questions, the test found her to be 'The Intern', a woman who is interested in sex, but expecting guys to come to her, and that success in a male is of the utmost importance.

Penny sent another message through. 'Care to defend your personality test?'

After a few minutes, Chris sent through, 'What do you mean?'

'90% slutty?'

'I wouldn't say "slutty", I'd say "adventurous"'.

Yuck, Penny thought. What a sleaze. She didn't know what to send back. Maybe it was time to move on from this guy. This online stuff was too weird. But at the same time, her heart was beating so fast.

'What about you,' he finally sent through. 'Care to defend your test miss I-want-the-guy-to-come-to-me?'

'Yeah, that's the way it should be,' she sent through.

'Why?'

'It's biological logic.'

'Fair enough. Let's meet up then.'

It was crunch time. Could Penny really meet up with someone she didn't even know? What if he was a murderer or something? But all her other single friends had resorted to online. She had to stick to her New Year's resolution. She would meet him in a public place and not give out her number.

The following night Penny found herself driving to Lygon Street, the Italian restaurant and café street of Melbourne. She was shaky—in her tummy, in her hands, everywhere—but it might have been the cold weather. Penny didn't want to exist on such days. She wanted to disappear to Greece and never return. She would have to organise a holiday soon. A visit to her grandmother would be nice.

Penny was no good at all this. She parked her car and took a deep breath. She repeated Clare's advice in her mind: 'Just remember, if you don't like him, it's okay. You are just having a coffee with another human being. Just a coffee. You'll be fine, darling, just fine.'

Penny stepped out of her car and walked. She hugged her jacket tight around her and made her way from the dimly lit Lygon back streets to the main thoroughfare. Then she noticed a man in front of her heading in the same direction, and she was pretty sure it was him. She hesitated a moment, stopped in her tracks, considered turning back, because he wasn't attractive, and plus what the hell was she doing there anyway? She took a deep breath to calm herself. She would go, just to satisfy her curiosity and nothing more. She would do the right thing, be polite, because he was Greek after all.

They had organised to meet outside Brunettis café, so when he reached it he stopped, turned around, and they kind of looked and each other, and smiled.

'Chris?'

'Penny?'

'Good to meet you,' she said, but thought *definitely no, does this guy ever shave? No, I need to have a quick coffee and go.*

'You too,' he smiled.

Brunettis café overflowed even on cold nights. There were no free tables inside or out and the situation wasn't looking promising at all.

'How about over there?' Chris said, pointing to a table next to a heater. The people sitting there were leaving. 'Why don't you grab that table and I'll go inside and order the coffees?'

'Okay.'

Chris asked what she wanted and she responded skinny latte.

After waiting nervously at the table for ten minutes, Chris approached with their hot drinks. Then the conversing began, mostly steered by Chris. Penny assessed him as he spoke. He looked different to his photo, but a little similar, possibly because he may have put on weight since the photo, or maybe he had aged. He had nice hazel eyes though. There was a moodiness to him, a darkness she wasn't able to articulate that intrigued her. Penny kept her gaze low when she spoke, or looked into the café, she was embarrassed to look directly at him. He took a genuine interest in her, asked many questions, and Penny answered openly, but then wondered if she was giving too much away, but then she thought it didn't matter, there was definitely no chemistry, and she'd probably never see him again.

'You live at home?' he asked when they got on the topic. 'Why? Surely as an accountant you can afford to move out.'

'I'll move out when I'm ready.'

'But don't your parents suffocate you?'

'No, I love my parents.'

'Yeah, so do I,' he laughed. 'I just don't want to fuck in the same house as them.'

Penny was speechless. How could he just drop the 'f' word like that? They didn't even know each other. She looked away.

'What? Did I say something to upset you?'

'No ... it's just ... nothing.'

He sat back in his chair, smirked like he found her oddly amusing.

'I don't buy into this online dating thing,' she continued.

'Yet here you are. It's just another way to meet people. I still meet people when I go out, or through my work.'

'It's an unnatural way of meeting someone. It's not normal.'

He laughed, but she didn't like his laugh. She was definitely not going to see him again. 'And what do you classify as "normal" in this technological world we live in?'

'Normal is you go out and you meet someone, you go on dates, you become boyfriend and girlfriend, you get married, you have kids. That's normal.'

'Sounds like you've got your whole life mapped out for you. I was married once. Long time ago. Married the kind of girl my parents dreamed of. Worked the kind of job my parents gloated about. It was sickening really.'

Penny was taken aback. Married? She didn't know what to say. Nothing was definitely going to happen between them now. She couldn't marry a divorced man. Divorced men were not on her list. They were used goods, and there was definitely something wrong with them, that's why they were divorced. Her heart was beating so fast she thought it was going to jump up her throat and start dancing on their table.

'I'm sorry to hear that,' she finally said.

'Don't be sorry.' Then he leaned into her, really close, and she could smell him—not aftershave, just his natural, manly scent—and she had to close her eyes, because he smelt so *good*. He said into her ear, 'I like being free. You should try it some day.'

Penny sat up and blurted. 'Well I don't think online dating is for me then.'

He took a moment. 'Well, it's getting late. Maybe we should head off.'

This took Penny by surprise. 'Okay.'

He walked her to her car in silence. She thanked him. Then he went in for a surprise hug, a tight one, and his embrace was comfortable, like when you come home late at night and all you want is your own pyjamas and your own bed, and for a second, something sparked, a vision of their first kiss flickered in her mind, but then reality set in, he was divorced, he was an artist who would never be able to provide for a family, he was just not her type physically either, so she pulled back, said goodnight, and went home.

It was Friday night in Melbourne and Penny couldn't believe she was walking from her office to a bar/restaurant on Flinders Lane for dinner and drinks with Chris. She wasn't expecting to hear from him again but he had texted her yesterday to ask if she was free. He had a meeting in the city and could meet if she wanted. Since she had nothing better to do, she agreed.

She found the place Chris had suggested, ordered a white wine, and waited. It was dimly lit, decked out in dark wood veneer, a bar that suited Chris's personality to a tee, she thought. Chris entered a short time later, dressed more smart-casual than their last meeting, shaven, but again Penny thought no way. They exchanged a quick kiss on the check, but then he confidently went in for the hug. They held on for a while.

'So here we are again,' he said.

'Yes, here we are.'

The conversation flowed freer this time, it was creamy, had texture, like the delicious, seafood linguini she was eating. He spoke more about his family, about his divorce six years ago, and his disillusionment at how fucked up ethnic families can be. Maybe it was the wine, but before Penny knew it their words were intertwining, and Penny was noticing his eyes, and how they shimmered with a depth that ignited her. He pulled her up and challenged her on things she said, and so did she to him. It was not a dynamic she had experienced before.

When Penny glanced at her watch—mid laughter—it was after midnight.

'I wasn't expecting to stay out this late. I guess I'll get a cab home.'

He smiled. 'I can take you home. I live in the city. We can walk to my place and I'll drive you home.'

Was Penny insane? She couldn't go home with this man.

'Um … okay,' the wine said.

It was a clear, crisp night, the stars were out and watching them. Bitter cold but no wind, so it was tolerable. When he noticed how cold she was he put his arm around her to warm her and she let him. They strolled like a couple, continued their conversation into other topics and then onto Chris's photography.

'I'd love to see some of your photos.'

'You'd have to come up to my apartment to do that,' he joked.

'Okay, why not?'

Inside Chris made two cups of tea. Penny tried not to look around too much but she couldn't help it. There were empty beer bottles on the bench, dirty dishes in the sink.

'Sorry, I wasn't expecting company,' he said, as he poured hot water into their mugs.

'Oh. It's fine.' He was a Greek man after all.

She walked along the hallway examining his photography on the walls. They were mostly portraits, but he was able to really capture depth and emotion through them. She wondered how much he sold his photographs for.

They had their tea on the living room sofa. While they talked, Penny eyed the guitar in the corner. 'You play?'

'Yeah.'

'I'd love to hear.'

He picked up the guitar, placed it on his knee and played. He sang too. Penny closed her eyes. It was as if the melody was unwrapping her. It was beautiful. She got so carried away with the sound, she didn't know how long he was playing for before he stopped. She opened her eyes. The guitar was on the floor and he was looking at her. They were looking at each other. And then, he abruptly brought his lips to hers—she pulled away, stunned. How could this be happening? she thought. How did she come to be here on his couch, in his apartment? But then, unable to resist, her gaze carefully lifted to his eyes, and that's all the encouragement he needed to kiss her again. This time their kiss was passionate, intense and deep, she couldn't catch her breath from it, their tongues swirling together, her head a maze of thoughts and questions and pressures she'd never be able to silence.

'I think I should get going,' she murmured mid-breath.

'Why?' he said, continuing to kiss her, their breathing quickening. He took hold of her face, kissed her deeper. They were igniting.

'No ...'

'Your entire body is saying you want to fuck me ... Don't you ever just relax and let your life unfold? Don't you just want to be free?'

They continued to kiss. Eventually, Chris led her to the bedroom. He scrambled to light some candles. They lay down on his bed. As he undressed her she trembled lightly. But when he reached for her breast, she pushed him away.

'What is it?'

'You can't touch my breasts.'

He raised his eyebrows. 'Why?'

'I just ... I don't ... I just do sex really, I've never done anything *else*.'

He held her in his arms and sighed. She rested her head on his naked chest. He kissed her head. 'Have you ever had a guy go down on you?'

'No.'

'Have you gone down on a guy?'

'No.'

'Have you ever come during sex, Penny?'

'I don't think so.'

'Do you want to?' He kissed her lips again, and then he moved to her neck, softly, used the tip of his tongue as he kissed her, tasted her. 'Do you want me to fuck you?' And more kissing, on the lips. 'Do you want me to make you come?' His tongue was in her mouth now, and she was breathing faster, so fast, his hand began to gently stroke one of her nipples, his other hand making its way down her underwear. 'Do you want me to run my tongue along your clit, and keep rubbing and licking until I make you come?' And he began rubbing there. 'You're so wet. You want this, Penny. Just let go, relax.'

She didn't want to move, yet she found herself wriggling out, but he held her, he held her. 'I want to but I can't,' and then she started to cry, she was crying.

He brought her into his embrace again. 'Do you want me to tie you up?'

'What do you mean?'

And then he was holding both her forearms, and she was shaking.

'Trust me. It'll help you. Okay?' He was looking her in the eyes, and for some reason she will never understand she nodded, and she said 'okay'.

She didn't know how he did it, but he tied her up on the bed like a starfish, using straps, and before she knew it he was running his tongue along her clit and she was fighting the straps—her orgasm—it was like a demon he was trying to exorcise from her soul.

His hands reached up and grabbed her breast, and he licked and licked, and she moaned and arched her back, fighting what was coming she said, 'I can't, I won't ...'

'You can. You want to. Just let it come. Let my tongue fuck you. I'll do this all night because you taste ... you taste so good. I can't wait to fuck you. I'm gonna fuck you so good, baby.'

And his words, and his tongue, the noises, the moaning, the groping, the pleasure, broke though some kind of wall within her mind and once she did she elevated to a place she'd never visited before, where there were no thoughts, and in this space, she kept climbing, and climbing until finally she released, broke, let go, and came.

Chris dropped Penny at home at around 3:30am. She had texted her mum earlier in the night to tell her she'd be home late. They were both quiet in the car. She asked if he could drop her a few doors down, just in case.

'I know the drill,' he said. 'I'm Greek remember.'

'But you're a guy.'

'I have a sister.'

'Ah.'

Before she opened the door she said. 'Was it good?'

He ran his hand through her hair. 'Amazing.'

'*Yia sou.*'

He reached for her, kissed her lips. '*Yia* ... See you soon.'

In her home, Penny showered, vigorously, thought of the priest judging her, then went straight to bed. She slept until three in the afternoon. When she woke she rang Shelly and told her what happened.

'Be careful not to get hurt,' Shelly said. But Penny didn't even know what that meant.

The next day, when she woke and still hadn't heard from him, Penny's emotions began to bubble like soup on a stove. Penny couldn't compartmentalise—she wasn't sure what she was feeling. Her muscles were sore from their sex, reminding her of what they did. And her situation didn't improve as the day progressed either. She spoke to Clare during her lunch break at work. Penny's mind was a muddle of misplaced brain cells. But the more she tried to put them in their correct order, the more scrabbled they became.

Penny spent the next few days moving through emotional states, from elated to lonely, to uncertain, to horny—she could barely concentrate at work, she was falling behind on house chores—she couldn't focus on anything. She exchanged a handful of texts with Chris, all initiated by her. Penny wasn't sure what was going on, if he liked her, or if it was just a one night thing. Penny finally found the courage to ask him out. They organised to meet at his place on Thursday night but he said he had an early start the next day so it couldn't be a late one, and instantly Penny thought, Oh, so I'm just a sex toy?

He greeted her at the front door, but he didn't hug or kiss her. He made cups of tea again but they sat on opposite sides of the living room this time. They spoke some every-day chatter, about work and the weather, and Penny noticed that his place was clean—no beer bottles, no dirty dishes.

'So ... that was weird the other night,' Penny said, braving the topic.

He smiled fondly, like he was recalling a distant memory. 'I think we both needed it.'

'You? According to your online profile you have sex all the time.'

'Not like that.'

They chatted some more and then the term 'fuck buddy' emerged, from Penny, because it was on her mind.

'From my experience,' he said, 'sex is more emotional for women, which is why women find it harder to have a fuck buddy.'

'So you can have sex and block out emotions?'

'Yes.'

'Did you block out emotions with me?'

'I don't want to answer that question.'

'Why?'

'Because I don't know you.' He looked away from her for a moment, annoyed. 'Look, obviously you've made some kind of judgment about me, that I'm some playboy. I wasn't expecting to have sex with you the other night, despite what you might think. I mean it was nice, but I just wanted to get to know you. I'm human too, Penny.'

'Okay.'

'It's getting late. I have to work tomorrow.' He stood.

'But I want to have sex.'

'But I told you I don't want a late one.'

'So you don't want to have sex with me?' Penny felt completely rejected. What was wrong with her that he didn't want to have sex with her? Was she not sexy enough?

'I wouldn't feel right about it.'

'But I want to.'

'I need to go to the bathroom.'

He went, and when he came back, Penny was sulking in her hands. He touched her hair. 'Why?'

'Please?'

He sighed, and then they were kissing. This time when they went to the bedroom to fuck, it was quick, furious—she came so hard she thought her body would shatter.

'You're killing me,' he murmured as he stammered from the bed after they were done.

'Am I going to see you this weekend?' she asked as he dressed.

'No, I'm busy.'

'Busy doing what? Seeing friends or fucking girls?'

He stopped a moment. 'Seeing friends.' He kissed her forehead.

When Penny saw the message through the dating website on Friday at work, all her suspicions and intuitions thundered through her. She had to quickly leave the office, said she was feeling unwell, and she cried all the way home on the tram, then in bed, for hours. Her mum knocked on her door to check on her. She told her she had a virus and her mum believed her. She wanted her parents to disappear.

In the message he had said they were too different and that he couldn't offer anymore than sex. He thought it best to end it now before they became emotionally entangled. He was taking his profile down from the dating website and wanted to lay low, figure out what he wanted. He thought it best they didn't contact each other for a while.

After some time, Penny forced herself from bed. She drew the curtains closed, threw on some daggy tracksuits, put on a DVD of *Seinfeld,* and went out to the kitchen to retrieve a fresh tub of cookies and cream ice-cream. Then she sat in her room, ate ice-cream, and cried.

Her mum knocked at the door. 'Are you okay?' she asked in Greek.

'Yes. Go away, please.'

She couldn't comprehend how upset she was about a guy she had only known a week, who she didn't even initially like. How did the power shift so swiftly? What did I do wrong? she thought. He didn't even tick a quarter of her boxes. So why was she so upset? What were her boxes again? She couldn't even remember.

That night, she dialled Chris's number.

'Hi,' he answered.

'Hi. I got your message.'

'Yeah. Sorry. It's just how I feel.'

'But why?'

'Because. And I don't have to justify it to you. I've got to go.'

'Why not? You fucked me.'

'So? That's sex.'

'So just tell me.'

'You're too fixed, Penny. I could never be with someone like you. You're judgemental, you're everything I can't stand about the Greeks. Everything. You think it's so hard being a woman in our culture? Try being a man! I will never subscribe to their ways again, or any ways you are inclined to subscribing to with your definition of normality. I don't want any of it. So if you want to just … be together for sex, I can do that, but nothing more.'

Penny didn't know what to say so she said. 'Okay. I'll go now.'

When Penny went into work a few weeks later, and a meeting was called, and they were all told that Clare had passed away, Penny quickly ran to the bathroom and threw up. A car accident they had said. It was instant. She didn't suffer. Penny sat on the toilet and cried and cried. She couldn't bear the pain inside her. It was like an avalanche, like being lost at sea in the wildest ocean. She felt as if her emotions were drowning her, and if she didn't grab onto something soon, she was going to go down with them.

Back at her desk, she texted Chris. *My friend died. I need sex. Can I come over?*

She stared at her phone for what seemed like an eternity, and then it beeped. *I'm sorry for your loss. Yes. Come over at 8:30pm. I'll make you forget.*

He greeted her at his door that night and held her. She cried in his arms. He had music playing. It had depth. Was sad.

'Sorry for your loss,' he said, and she cried and cried and cried.

'I don't want to die ... I don't want to be alone. I want a husband. I want a partner.'

He kissed her head. 'We're all alone, Penny.'

She cried harder. 'No ...'

'Yes. Even when you have someone, you're still alone.'

She began convulsing. 'It's not true ...'

'It is.'

He began running his fingers through her hair. He kissed her, deeply. He tasted like wine, and she imagined him drinking one glass after another, so he could build up the courage to do what he was doing. Their bodies became infused with European jazz, Byzantine chant, the improvisatory passages of the music guiding their hands and bodies as they swayed to the sax. She cried in his mouth. He drank her tears, like they were his life source. She trembled in his arms.

'I want to fuck you,' he said.

She pushed against him, and he pushed back, both pushing for power, wanting the control, wanting it their way, but it was not theirs to have. It was the moment that lay claim to the power. Penny pushed against him, and cried, and cried, for all she wanted was for him to hold her, for him to be someone that loved her, someone of importance in her life.

Their love-making quickly became rough, picked up pace and fervour as the music progressed and intensified with the percussion, the anger of the vocals, Chris was angry, impatient, drew power from her vulnerability. He lay her on the bed, his tongue, pleasuring her, but his words *You are alone* stabbed at her chest like icicles, yet there were waves and waves of unstoppable ecstasy and euphoria, tumbling and receding, tumbling and receding.

'I love my friend so much,' she said.

'You love to love,' he said. 'You love to love.'

And then she came, she came so hard. He quickly crawled up to her.

'I want you to suck my cock,' he said. He grabbed her by the hair.

'No way. I've never done that.'

But he pushed her down. 'Suck it.'

'No.'

'You need to go there.'

'Fuck you, Chris! Fuck you.' How many tears was she going to cry? The sex was stabbing at every emotional particle in her being. She fought him with every ounce of her strength, but then she just couldn't anymore, she just couldn't. So she went down, he was on his back, and she went down there and took him into her mouth.

'Oh, God,' he muttered. 'That's so good.' He held her there.

His words made her want to suck it more. So she did. And he moaned louder. She touched herself between her legs. She was so wet. She was so powerful, she felt powerful, and womanly, having him in her mouth.

'Stop, I'll come. Fuck. Let me fuck you. I want to fuck you.'

He climbed on top of her. 'What do you want me to do?' he asked.

And they were looking into each other's eyes.

'Hold me.'

'I'm holding you.'

'I want to be with you,' she said.

'You can never own me. I can't be loved.'

And so they fucked, like this, many times into the night, until she fell asleep in his arms.

Chris took her home in the early hours again. They both joked that they wouldn't be going in to work tomorrow. They were too exhausted to say much beyond that. Every bone in her body ached. But it was a good ache.

Penny went inside, had a shower and slept. When she woke the next morning she went straight onto her laptop to search for a house to buy.

Acknowledgements

The inspiration for these stories was born in Ania Walwicz's short story class and for whom I will always be indebted for showing me a door to myself and my voice. Ania, you never judged and you always encouraged me to listen to myself *only*, even to your final days when we walked in Carlton Gardens. It took me a long time to listen. I miss you greatly. You will always be my teacher. Thank you for believing in me.

Thank you to Ed Wright and the team and Puncher and Wattmann for believing in this collection enough to publish it. Thank you to Christos Tsiolkas for ongoing mentorship and career support, for seeing something in me and encouraging me to pursue a career in writing despite the cultural hurdles. To Les Zigomanis, for editorial support, career guidance, and for believing in me and always pushing me to keep going even when I have wanted to throw in the towel. To David Cameron, thank you for your ongoing friendship, love and support and for accepting me for who I am, for reading multiple drafts of my collection and providing feedback, and always being my rock. Thank you to my family for their support. To Lisa Tribuzio, Alexandros Demetriades and anyone else who I have accidentally forgotten. And last but not least, to my daughter, my light, my true love, whose emergence into my life had me questioning everything. You gave me the strength and courage to find myself so I could one day inspire you. I hope I have.

About the author

Koraly Dimitriadis is a bestselling Cypriot-Australian writer and performer. She is the author of the poetry books *Love and Fuck Poems* (also in Greek), *Just Give Me The Pills* and *She's Not Normal.* Her poems have been translated and published in journals in Polish, Czech, Greek and Greek-Cypriot. Her short stories, essays and poems have been published in *Southerly, Etchings, Overland, Unusual Works, Social Alternatives, Meanjin, Solid Air* (UQP), *Resilience* (Ultimo/Mascara), *Foyer* (UK) and others. Koraly's poetry films have been shortlisted for prizes, screened at festivals and televised, including on SBS. Koraly has performed internationally, including at The Poetry Café (London) and The Bowery (New York). Koraly's poetic theatre monologue, *I say the wrong things all the time* premiered at La Mama and she has performed in Outer Urban Projects's Poetic License (Melbourne Writers Festival, 45 Downstairs, Darebin Arts). Koraly's essays/opinion articles have been published widely across Australia in publications such as *ABC, SBS, The Age, SMH, Women's Agenda, The Saturday Paper, Neos Kosmos,* with international publications in *The Independent* (UK), *Shondaland, The Guardian, The Washington Post, The Today show* (USA) and *Al Jazeera.* For her fiction manuscript, *We Never Said Goodbye,* Koraly was awarded residencies at UNESCO City of Literature (Krakow), Wheeler Centre, Chantilly, HOANI (Cyprus) and Moreland Council. Koraly holds a diploma in professional writing/editing (RMIT) and a double degree in accounting/computing (Monash). She is a mentor, has spoken on panels, run workshops, and has been interviewed on television and radio including ABC's *The Conversation Hour with Jon Faine.* Koraly is currently developing her first creative non-fiction book, *Not Till You're Married.*
www.koralydimitriadis.com

Acknowledgements

"Blood-red numbers" first published in [Untitled] (Busybird Press), Issue 3, 2010.

"The Bookshop", first published in *The Brunswick Strip: a series of 8 erotic stories* (Little Raven), 2013, and then again in *A Storytelling of Ravens: The Best of Little Raven Publishing* (Little Raven), 2014.

"The Recipe" selected for the Overland masterclass, 2009, longlisted for the FISH Prize (Ireland), 2011, first published in *Southerly Journal: Writing Disability* (Brandl & Schlesinger), Volume 76, Number 2, 2016.

"The Mother Must Die", first published in the Mascara anthology, *Resilience* (Ultimo), 2022.

Printed in Australia
Ingram Content Group Australia Pty Ltd
AUHW020924200924
400125AU00001B/2

9 781923 099340